DEA...

Fargo heard nothing
He felt a sharp pain i
instant. He put a hand to his face and felt the
flow of red.

A wave of dizziness swept over him, and sent
the world into a spinning grayness. He shook
his head, and was able to see the rifleman
standing on top of the ledge, and other horsemen coming out of the crevices toward him.
The figures seemed to move in a haze, wavy
and indistinct. His eyes closed and he lay
limp, but he could still hear the faint voices.

"He's dead," one of them said.

"For sure," a second agreed.

"Throw him into the gully," another commanded.

Fargo wanted to rise, turn, kick out, but his
body lay powerless. He felt himself roughly
lifted, flung into the empty air, and lost the
last of his consciousness as he hit the first
ledge. He wasn't able to hear the killers laugh
as they turned away from their latest victim.

Skye Fargo wasn't about to die, though. Not
when he was mad enough to kill . . .

**BE SURE TO READ THE OTHER
THRILLING NOVELS IN THE EXCITING
TRAILSMAN SERIES!**

THE TRAILSMAN

#194

MONTANA STAGE

by

Jon Sharpe

A SIGNET BOOK

SIGNET
Published by the Penguin Group
Penguin Putnam Inc., 375 Hudson Street,
New York, New York 10014, U.S.A.
Penguin Books Ltd, 27 Wrights Lane,
London W8 5TZ, England
Penguin Books Australia ltd,
Ringwood, Victoria, Australia
Penguin Books Canada Ltd, 10 Alcorn Avenue,
Toronto, Ontario, Canada M4V 3B2
Penguin Books (N.Z.) Ltd, 182-190 Wairau Road,
Auckland 10, New Zealand

Penguin Books Ltd, Registered Offices:
Harmondsworth, Middlesex, England

First published by Signet, an imprint of Dutton Signet,
a member of Penguin Putnam Inc.

First Printing, February, 1998
10 9 8 7 6 5 4 3 2

Copyright © Jon Sharpe, 1998
All rights reserved

The first chapter of this book originally appeared in *Bullets and Bridles*,
the one hundred ninety-third volume in this series.

 REGISTERED TRADEMARK—MARCA REGISTRADA

Printed in Canada

The Trailsman

Beginnings . . . they bend the tree and they mark the man. Skye Fargo was born when he was eighteen. Terror was his midwife, vengeance his first cry. Killing spawned Skye Fargo, ruthless, cold-blooded murder. Out of the acrid smoke of gunpowder still hanging in the air, he rose, cried out a promise never forgotten.

The Trailsman they began to call him all across the West: searcher, scout, hunter, the man who could see where others only looked, his skills for hire but not his soul, the man who lived each day to the fullest, yet trailed each tomorrow. Skye Fargo, the Trailsman, and the seeker who could take the wildness of a land and the wanting of a woman and make them his own.

*It began in Montana,
in the Beaverhead foothills,
the strange story of the
vanishing stagecoach, where death
and greed were the unseen passengers . . . .*

1

The big man snapped his eyes open and let a soft oath escape his lips as the sudden clatter intruded upon the peaceful quiet of the glen. He sat up in the thicket of yellow-flowered hop cover, his hand automatically dropping to the butt of the big Colt at his hip. His lake blue eyes peered up at the road that ran alongside the tall sandstone rocks some fifty yards away and as he watched, the stagecoach burst into view. A four-horse team running all-out and driverless, sent the coach careening wildly along the curves of the road.

"Shit," he swore aloud as he leaped to his feet and saw the stage gather even more speed on a short stretch of straight road. No mud-wagon or light-bodied coach, he saw, but a full Concord with a front and rear boot, the classic of stagecoaches, the finest of the coachmaker's art and the heart of transportation in this wild land.

Running forward, Skye Fargo dug his heels into the firm ground as he ran to where the Ovaro grazed on a field of panic grass, made a vaulting leap into the saddle, and sent the horse into an instant gallop. A quick glance at the stagecoach let him see the wagon careening on two wheels as it disappeared around a curve. He hadn't seen any passengers but they were probably at the bottom of the coach, clinging on for dear life or perhaps already knocked unconscious. When he neared the rocks, Fargo kept the Ovaro just below the road along a flat stretch as he galloped past the coach. Seeing a narrow passage appear to his left, he sent the pinto into it and let it take him up to the road just as the four-horse team came thundering around the curve. Slowing, Fargo let the runaway horses pass him on the narrow width of road. When the coach came abreast of him, keeping his thighs tight around the horse, he leaned out and closed one hand on the iron rail that rimmed the driver's seat.

Gathering every muscle in his powerful body, he half leaped, half pulled himself through the air, twisting his body as he did. Slamming into the side of the coach, he got an arm around the iron rail, then a leg, and flung himself sideways onto the driver's seat. Turning, he saw the next curve coming up, the stage rocking back and forth from side to side. It wouldn't make the sharpness of the curve, he knew, and he grabbed hold of the wildly flapping reins. He pulled hard on the two outside horses, making them turn in and slow the other two. The team began to rein in as he took the curve, slowing enough to negotiate the dangerous bend. Pulling steadily, he continued to slow the heavy stagecoach as it came out of the curve and finally brought it to a halt on a straight stretch of the road.

The horses blew air as they breathed hard, glad to end their panic-stricken, headlong flight. Fargo swung from the coach and pulled the door open.

The furrow dug into his brow as he stared into the stage and saw the emptiness that greeted him. Possibilities leaped into his head at once. Had the horses bolted when the passengers had been outside, he wondered. Had they been thrown out during the wild ride? Or had the stage been empty all along. The last didn't sit right. Nobody ran an empty stage across this territory. It didn't pay to go without a stage at least half full. He went to the front boot and pulled the canvas aside. A single suitcase stared back at him from inside the boot. He moved past the stage to check the rear boot, where he saw a woman's traveling bag. But the two pieces were enough to tell him there had been passengers. Returning to the body of the coach, he leaned inside and spied the handkerchief on the floor, wedged against the inner door.

Small, with an embroidered border, it was unquestionably a woman's handkerchief. Two passengers definitely, probably more, Fargo guessed. But what had happened to them? He couldn't go back looking for them. The stage could have come from anywhere in the territory. But the thought slid through his mind. If he couldn't find where it had been, maybe he could find out where it was going. His eyes went to the team. Horses that pulled a stage on a regular run quickly learned the route, often better than many a driver. They could go it on their own with a combination of memory and instinct. He surveyed the horses and saw that they had calmed down, though two were still lathered. Pulling himself into the driver's seat of the stage, he took the reins again and gave the team the order to move with a gentle touch. They went on and he kept them at a walk, then at a slow trot, then he sat back and let the team go on without direction from him.

The Ovaro followed along, as he knew it would, and Fargo watched the horses move along the road between the sandstone rocks. When the road moved downward, it turned onto scrub brush prairie land and came to another road, Fargo sat up straight as the horses unhesitatingly took the second road. He held the reins loosely and the team went down the second road that cut across land studded with clusters of burr oak and rock. The road led over a stretch of plains heavy with gray-green sagebrush and when another road appeared he watched the horses take it without even slowing. Flocks of crows and Bullock's orioles flew overhead as the stage went on and Fargo saw two lakes in the distance. The road rose into low, rolling hills and in the distance he saw tall rock formations rise up. Suddenly, the team veered from the road and quickened its speed as it rode through low scrub brush. Fargo saw the small cluster of buildings rise up.

The team pulled into what was plainly a way station of a square building and two sheds. They instantly came to a halt alongside a long water trough as a man hurried from the building. Wearing trousers and a checkered vest, he halted as Fargo swung to the ground. He frowned from under thinning hair. "Who are you, mister?" he asked.

"Fargo. Skye Fargo," the Trailsman answered.

"Where's Willie Matson?" the man asked.

"He the usual driver?" Fargo returned.

"That's right," the man said.

"He wasn't with the stage. Neither were the passengers. It was a runaway all by itself," Fargo said. "I stopped it, let the horses find their way."

"What happened?" the man questioned.

"I don't know. Thought I'd get some answers here," Fargo said. "No driver, no passengers. You tell me."

"Jesus," the man said, staring at the coach. "This is only a way station, mister. You take the stage on to Bolton Flats. That's where it was headed."

"Bolton Flats?"

"Other side of those high rocks. There's a road through. You'll see it. Mr. Collins will want to see you. It's his stage line. I know he'll pay you for bringing it in," the man said.

Fargo thought for a moment. He didn't care a damn about pay for bringing in the wagon. But his curiosity was aroused. Besides, the quiet of his day had been thoroughly shattered. "All right, I'll take the stage in. Water the horses," he said and the man nodded almost eagerly. Fargo stepped into the house, found a tin pitcher of cool water, and refreshed himself. When he returned to the big Concord the horses had been rubbed down and watered.

"Collins. Buzz Collins," the man said. "The depot master will tell you where he is." Fargo nodded, climbed onto the coach, and sent it rolling forward. He set an easy pace for the team, and finally reached the rocks and found a road leading between the towering stones. The road curved and climbed and soon Fargo found himself high into the rocks, mostly granite and basalt and honey-combed with narrow crevices on both sides of the road. The sound of the horses and the stage echoed through the stone canyons, obliterating all other noises. Fargo heard nothing until the shot exploded. He felt the sharp pain in his temple at the same instant. When he put a hand to his face he could feel the flow of red coursing down his cheek.

A wave of dizziness swept over him at once, sending the world into a spinning grayness. Fargo shook his head and winced in pain but the world returned, long enough for him to see the rifleman stop at one of the high rocks, then other horsemen coming out of the crevices toward him. He pulled on the reins to bring the stage to a halt as he felt himself toppling from the seat. Another shot rang out as he hit the ground. He gasped in pain as he lay half on his side on the gravelly road. He could see the figures moving toward him in a haze, wavy and indistinct, their voices faint. His eyes closed and he lay limp, hardly breathing, a line of red sliding down the side of his face from his temple. But he could still hear the faint voices.

"We got the damn stage," one voice said.

"No damn thanks to you," another voice said.

"How did I know they'd bolt?" the other voice said.

"Hell, you shot right next to them, you damn fool," the other said.

"What about him? He's dead," the first voice said.

"Throw him over the side," the other said.

14

Fargo wanted to rise, turn, and kick out, but his body lay powerless, refusing to respond to his silent urgings, and his temple burned as if on fire. The dizziness stayed, closing out the world as he barely breathed. He felt himself lifted and flung into the air. He lost the last of his consciousness as he hit the first ledge, then the second. The world vanished completely. He was unaware of how many jutting rocks he struck as he fell, nor was he aware of finally hitting the bottom. He lay for uncounted, unknown hours, immersed in a void, without sound, sight, or sensation, dead so far as he knew, so far as anyone knew.

Then suddenly there was something. He didn't know what, but something, a flicker of awareness. Slowly, it took on substance and became more than a flicker. Awareness took on definition and became a cold hardness. Sensation. But the dead didn't feel anything. The dead didn't know sensation. They didn't reason, detect, come to conclusions. The dead weren't aware. He was alive, Fargo realized, the thought slowly sliding through him. A sound came from his throat, a strange, gargled sound. To Fargo it was laughter, wonderful, consuming laughter. He lay still, listening to the soft hiss of his breath and reveling in the sound. Finally, he tried moving the fingers of one hand and felt them curl and tighten. He moved his arm next, stretched it out and followed with one leg, then the other, each movement an affirmation. He was alive. He pulled his eyelids open, blinked, and let his eyes adjust to the light and saw that the sun was still on the land. He slowly pushed to his feet, ignoring the pain that shot through his body, along the side of his temple.

But he knew he had been unconscious for hours. The dried state of the blood along his face told him that much. He peered up along the side of the rocks at the edge of the road high above. But the cliffside wasn't sheer, he saw. Ledges and clusters of uneven rock jutted out all over it. Wincing with the pain of bruised ribs and back, he began to pull himself up along the rocks. He moved slowly, gasping with each pull of his sore and strained muscles. It seemed to take forever before he reached the top and he had to stop often along the way. But finally he pulled himself over the edge of the road and lay there as he let his breath return. He pushed to one knee, whistled, waited, and whistled again and then again. When he heard the sound of hooves on the stone of the road, he rose to his feet and stretched out one arm as the Ovaro came around the curve.

He leaned against the warm strength of the great jet black neck for a moment and then ran his hands over the snow white midsection and jet hindquarters. "Give me up for lost, old friend?" he asked. "So did I." The horse shook his head and snorted in greeting and Fargo pulled himself into the saddle. The sun was sliding behind the distant peaks and he let his thoughts begin to assemble what little he knew about the attackers. They had assumed the first shot had killed him and were in too much of a hurry to make sure. The fragments of their conversation swam back through his mind. Their chief concern had been the stage. They had stopped it someplace not that far away. Then the horses had bolted from a shot. Fargo let himself guess what had happened then. They'd been left with the passengers on their hands. They had to do something about them before they could take off after the stage. Tie and gag them? That'd take time. To shoot them would be faster. But they'd still have to drag the bodies out of sight.

Either way, they hadn't been able to immediately chase after the stage and the runaway team had continued its headlong flight. That's when he had first seen it, Fargo thought back. But one question hung in his thoughts. If they had stopped the stage to rob the passengers, why had they gone chasing after the coach at all? It didn't make sense. He couldn't come up with an answer to that but he had reconstructed a loose idea of what had happened before he'd first seen the runaway stage. His eyes went to the road and he saw that they had managed to turn the stage around. Wheelmarks showed they had taken the stage back the way it had come. He walked the Ovaro after the wheelmarks. Not only were there a lot of questions that needed answering, but perhaps people that needed rescuing. Besides, they had tried to kill him. He wasn't about to forget that.

Fargo followed the road back until it curved downward, leaving the high hills, and moving onto the flatland, where he circled the way station and rode up into the low hills, where he'd first seen the stage. He followed the wheelmarks and saw the road curve downward onto flatland heavy with forests of white fir interspersed with granite ridges. But the last of the day was sliding away, the blanket of night quickly rolling over the land. Trailing would be at an end in the dark and he found a spot between two large firs, unsaddled the Ovaro, and set out his bedroll. Before he stretched out, he used the water of his canteen to clean the caked blood from his temple and the side of his face. He ate a stick of dried beef from his saddlebag and as he lay down, two questions continued to stab at him. Why had chasing after the stage been so damn important and what had happened to the passengers? The questions only went away when sleep came to shut them out.

He woke with the new day, his body less sore after a good night's sleep and he returned to tracking the wheel marks. He counted some six or so horses accompanying the stagecoach, but now, as he rode, he sought more than trail marks. His eyes scanned the terrain on both sides of the road, searching for trees pushed aside, brush disturbed, unnatural rock groups. But he saw nothing to investigate and the road grew more indistinct, becoming part of the land where suddenly thick growths of serviceberry and dogwood emerged. A few hundred yards further, the trail marks were gone.

Frowning, Fargo swung from the saddle and proceeded on foot, the frown digging deeper into his brow. There were no wheelmarks in the grama grass, no hoofprints nearby, nothing. The stage had disappeared. Only stages didn't just disappear. The trail had been covered up, carefully and expertly. No stage and, more importantly, no passengers. But they hadn't just vanished. They were somewhere, the passengers alive, he hoped, a grim hope, he admitted. Perhaps he could pick up signs, marks, a complete elimination of a trail was almost impossible. But they could have gone off in any direction. It would take too long to completely scour the land and he was growing fearful that time was important. He had to know more about the stage, where it had originated, about those who'd taken passage on it. Maybe then he'd have a chance to find the answers.

He turned the Ovaro around and put the horse into a fast trot. The stage was going to Bolton's Landing. Maybe he'd find what he needed there. Maybe a waiting relative could help. Maybe Buzz Collins, owner of the stage line could offer something. One thing was becoming terribly clear. It hadn't been an ordinary stagecoach holdup. Passengers were robbed, sometimes killed, in ordinary holdups. But the stages were left. They weren't chased down, then made to vanish. There was more here. But what and why? The questions rode with him as he drove the big Ovaro harder.

2

Bolton Flats turned out to be a larger town than he'd expected when he reached it under the early-afternoon sun. The unpaved main street bustled with wagon traffic, mostly one-horse Owensboro farm wagons, cut-under spring wagons, and heavier seedbed wagons, but he noted a good sprinkling of buckboards and surreys. He rode through the street, took in the usual saloon, blacksmith shop, barbershop, and general store. But he also noted a sizable boarding inn, a meeting hall, and a bank, all signs of a town that had set down roots. He had reached the center of town when he spotted the unpainted wooden building with the sign lettered across the top: STAGE DEPOT. As he drew up before it he saw the small knot of people waiting outside. A quick glance showed him two women, one with a six-year-old boy, and two men. They peered down the street, anxiety on each of their faces as a man stepped from the building. He wore a vest over his white shirt and Fargo saw the ticket punch hanging from his belt. He peered down the street with the others, frowning.

"You the stationmaster?" Fargo asked and the man nodded back. "You waiting for a stage?" Fargo questioned.

"The stage from Wyoming. It was due in yesterday," the stationmaster said.

"We all are," a man in the small group put in. "You know anything about it, mister?"

Fargo took in a well-dressed man in a brown suit with a stiff, high collar and a necktie, long sideburns on his concerned face, graying hair, a square head, a face that hadn't spent a lot of time outdoors. "It won't be coming in," Fargo said, including everyone in his quick glance.

"You see it?" the stationmaster asked.

"You could say that," Fargo answered.

"It have a breakdown?" the man asked.

"It disappeared." Fargo said. Glancing at the others, he saw shock, alarm, and incredulousness sweep their faces. One, a young woman with a pretty, round-cheeked face, stared up at him in disbelief. But it was the stationmaster's jaw that dropped the furthest.

"Jesus," the man gasped. "Look, mister, you better go see Mr. Collins. Right away."

"I was going to do that," Fargo said.

"Wait," the pretty-faced young woman said and Fargo took in brown eyes and brown hair that echoed the eyes in tone, a small nose, and round, full lips, a face both determined and pretty. A traveling dress of green cotton cut high at the neck covered a balanced figure that was more neat than sensuous. "What do you mean the stage disappeared?" she questioned.

"Just what I said," Fargo answered.

"That doesn't make any sense." She frowned.

"I didn't say it did," Fargo replied.

21

"What about the passengers," the man in the brown suit cut in.

"They weren't on it when I saw it," Fargo said.

"Enough talk, mister. You get to Buzz Collins," the stationmaster interrupted. "End of town, big, long shed with a house next to it."

"No, wait. We want to know more. Please," the young woman said as Fargo started to move the Ovaro forward.

"I don't know more," Fargo said, seeing the terrible anxiety in their faces. "I'll stop back," he said and spurred the pinto into a trot. He reached the end of town in minutes and saw the long shed at once. A large circle of land alongside it held a collection of spare wagon parts, extra wheels, shafts, axles, and even a section of coach body propped up on boards. The house beside the shed reflected quiet opulence, heavy stone with log trim, a flagstone terrace, and a slate roof. Fargo dismounted and the door opened quickly at his knock. A woman gazed back at him, a strikingly attractive woman, short, onyx hair that made pale white skin seem even paler, a thin nose, and arching eyebrows. But it was her eyes that held him, large and round, they seemed to smolder with a pale blue fire. A tall body was clothed in a white, tailored shirt and black riding jodhpurs. Full breasts pressed the white shirt out with smooth fullness. He guessed her to be somewhere just the sunny side of thirty. "Looking for Buzz Collins," Fargo said as the pale blue eyes moved over him with interest and approval.

"What do you want with him. I'm his sister, Leah Collins," the woman said.

"It's about his stage, the one due in yesterday," Fargo said.

"Buzz, come here," the woman called over her shoulder. "It's about the stage." Fargo heard footsteps hurrying and the man appeared. Tall, broad-shouldered, younger than the woman, he had her thin nose and onyx hair, but his eyes were darker, nervous, darting, a sharp-edged quality to his face.

"You know something about my stage?" he asked aggressively.

"I know it's gone, disappeared," Fargo said and Buzz Collins stared back as his face drained of color.

"What else do you know, mister?" Buzz Collins asked.

"Not much more," Fargo said and told the man what had happened. When he finished, the color had returned to Buzz Collins's face, turning it a deep red.

"Goddamn, goddamn," the man said with a hiss. "This is the fourth stage I've lost. Nobody saw hide nor hair of the other three. They just disappeared. I thought I was going crazy. Nobody could understand it. They were coming up with all kinds of crazy explanations."

"People were even talking about an evil spirit the Shoshone put on the stages," Leah cut in.

"But now, you saw this one taken. This puts a different light on things. They're being taken, hijacked, goddammit," Collins said.

"Why?" Fargo asked.

"I don't know why. I only know I've got to get them back, this one and the other three, all of them," Collins said. "Now there's something to go on. What's your name, mister?"

"Fargo, Skye Fargo."

Buzz Collins frowned as he turned the name in his mind. "I've heard of you," he muttered.

"Some call me the Trailsman," Fargo said.

Collins's eyes widened. "Sure, that's it. I was in Kansas a few years back when you were breaking trail for the Abernathy spread. Jesus, you came to the right place at the right time. I'll pay you to find that stage and the others, pay you real well. Six thousand, eight if you find them real fast."

It was Fargo's eyes that widened this time. "That's a powerful lot of money," he said.

"It is but I want those stages back. They're first-class Concords, made by Abbot and Downing. I want you to start in the morning. You're the man for the job. Half the money up front," Collins said.

Fargo studied the man's sharp-edged face. Collins was agitated and excited, not unlike a drowning man who suddenly sees a life preserver. Yet there was an icy ruthlessness to the man. "You've never said a word about the passengers," Fargo remarked.

"Forget the damn passengers. Stages are a lot harder to come by than passengers," Collins flung back, as he turned and strode away. "Wait here," he said.

Fargo felt Leah's hand on his arm and saw that she had picked up the disapproval in his face at her brother's words. "He didn't mean that," she said.

"You could've fooled me," Fargo replied.

24

"Buzz is very distraught. He's been beside himself since the first stage disappeared," she said.

"You always make excuses for him?" Fargo asked with a half smile.

"People often say things when they're upset they wouldn't say otherwise," she said.

"And they often say what they really feel when they're upset," he countered.

She gave a half shrug. "Trust me on this," she said and her hand stayed on his arm as Collins returned.

"Thought I might have the cash on hand but I'll go to the bank in the morning," Collins said.

"I didn't agree to anything. I'll have to think some on this," Fargo said.

"Six thousand shouldn't take too much thinking," Collins snapped.

"Spend the night at the inn, sleep on it, Fargo," Leah put in soothingly. "We'll pick up the bill. We owe you that much for telling us what you found."

"Fair enough," Fargo said and Leah linked her arm in his as he turned to go.

"I'll see Fargo to his horse," she said to her brother.

"Six thousand," Collins called after them.

Fargo felt the soft warmth of the side of one breast as Leah held his arm until they were beside the Ovaro. "Buzz hasn't learned that money doesn't buy everything or everyone," Leah Collins said. "It'll take time."

"You've learned that?" Fargo asked.

"Oh yes," she said. "Get a good night's rest and we'll talk come morning." She let his arm go and he swung onto the Ovaro, nodding to her as he rode away. The frown clung to his brow as he walked the pinto through town and saw the day beginning to slide away.

The meeting with Buzz Collins continued to bother him. It was not just the man's complete indifference to the fate of the passengers. Collins was plainly a man wrapped tight as a coiled wire. He'd kept curling and uncurling his fingers all the time they talked. There was a strange desperation in his need to get the stagecoaches back. He'd offered more than six thousand dollars to get the stages. He could buy brand-new ones for that kind of money, even from the Abbot and Downing coachmakers. It didn't figure. There was something more. Fargo grunted. Yet it was the kind of money a man would be a damn fool to turn down. And he had a score to settle, Fargo reminded himself as he reached the depot. The small knot of figures were still waiting there and the man in the brown suit stepped forward.

"You find out anything?" he asked.

"Nothing I didn't know. Collins asked me to find his stages," Fargo said.

"Finding the passengers is more important," the pretty-faced young woman snapped.

"I won't disagree with you but everybody has their own idea of what's important," Fargo said.

"Look, I'm Rod Harris," the man in the brown suit said. "My business associate, Steven Tinsdale, was bringing terribly important documents to me. I must get those papers. I have to find Steven and his things."

"I'm Melanie Carter," the young woman said.

"My cousin, Lucy, was on that stage. Finding her is the most important thing in the world to me."

The woman with the little boy spoke up. "My husband was on that stage. I want to find him," she said with heart-twisting simplicity. "My name is Winifred Bivins. My husband's Fred."

"Roger Abel's my brother. He was bringing vital family documents. I've got to find him and his things," the second man said.

"Human life is more important than any stagecoach," Melanie Carter said righteously.

"I'm not arguing," Fargo said.

"But you're going to look for the stage. You should be looking for the passengers," she said, reproach in her voice.

"Haven't decided that, either," Fargo said.

"You're the one connection to it all. You just going to walk away?" Melanie Carter said. The determination he had seen in her pretty, round-cheeked face was definitely there, Fargo thought to himself silently.

"Right now I'm going to get me a meal and some sleep," he said.

"That's no answer," she snapped.

"It's the only one you're getting," Fargo said and moved the pinto forward. Glancing back, he saw Melanie Carter and the others in a huddle and felt sorry for them. Three other stages had vanished. Their passengers hadn't turned up anywhere. It didn't bode well for those who'd been on this last stage.

Fargo slowed and halted in front of the saloon as night descended. He went in, had a buffalo sandwich, and washed it down with bourbon. The

27

boarding inn was his next stop. He took a small but neat room, pulled off his shirt and boots and stretched out on a good bed. He lay still, a kerosene lamp turned on low, and let his thoughts form themselves. Almost an hour had passed when they pushed the decision on him. He'd take Buzz Collins's offer, despite the misgivings he had about it. His own curiosity gave it the final push. He had to give it a try and he was about to turn on his side when the knock came at the door, soft yet firm. He swung from the bed, opened the door, and his brows lifted when he saw Leah Collins there.

"May I come in?" she asked.

"Sure," Fargo said as she passed him. "Didn't expect visitors."

"I like to do the unexpected," Leah said as her pale blue eyes slowly moved across Fargo's naked torso and took in the muscled contours of his powerful frame.

"You come here to do some more convincing?" Fargo asked.

"Guess so," she said. "I've never seen Buzz so upset as he's been over these strange disappearances of the stages. I've been terribly upset myself for him. I'm afraid I've been a big sister too long. Can't shake the habit."

"Nothing wrong with that," Fargo said.

"Been doing it ever since our folks died. The stagecoach line has been the first project Buzz has done real well at and I feel strongly for him. I want you to find the stages for him. I want to help you agree to do it."

"Help me?"

"I know money won't decide you all by itself. You're not that kind. I can tell," Leah Collins said. "I've come to add something else, call it a bonus." Her hand went to the top button of the tailored shirt and she flicked it open.

"You think that'll make me decide?" he asked and saw the pale blue challenge in her eyes.

"I'd hope so," she said. Her hand paused at the second button and waited there. He smiled as thoughts leaped through his mind. She wanted to help her brother. It wouldn't be fair to deny her that satisfaction, he told himself. And perhaps there was something else. Perhaps helping her brother was a convenient excuse for something she wanted to do. If so, it'd be downright ungentlemanly to deny her that. He'd not say he had already decided to take the offer. It was the only proper thing to do.

"I imagine it would," he said. A tiny smile touched her lips and her fingers opened the second button. The third followed and in moments the tailored shirt hung open. She pulled it off and he took in full breasts, nicely curved, perhaps a trifle long. But the pale white skin gave them a shimmering quality and made each tiny nipple seem redder than it was, while each circling areole glowed with a pale pink. Her breasts swayed gently as she pushed away the black jodhpurs and he took in a long waist that curved into a sensuous little belly. Below, a dense triangle seemed jet black against the pale white skin. Thighs perhaps a little heavy, nonetheless moved gracefully as she lowered herself onto the bed, reached out for him, and helped him shed the few clothes he wore.

He came against her, the pale white skin surprisingly hot and her eyes, while they remained pale blue, took on a new intensity, a kind of fire without flame. "Ah, ah, ah yes . . . yes," Leah Collins whispered as his mouth moved down to one breast and caressed the very red little nipple, his tongue moving back and forth across the soft-firm tip. "Yes, yes . . . more, oh, more," Leah murmured, twisting and pushing her breast deeper into his mouth. "Harder . . . aaaaah, yes, harder." She gasped and he drew in the pale white mound, sucking harder and biting down harder, causing Leah to utter a half cry, half laugh of pure pleasure.

Her hands moved across his back, over his shoulders, pressing, pushing, digging in. "Ah, aaaaaaah, ah God," she cried out as his hand traced a trackless path down across her abdomen, down to the soft convexity of her belly exploring the elliptical little indentation, moving down to the edge of the jet triangle. "Aaaaiiieeee, Jesus, yes, yes," she half screamed as he pushed through the wiry tendrils, rubbing against the bulge beneath where the Venus mound pushed upward. His hand slid downward and her thighs fell open, closed, and open again, the flesh sending its own message. His hand pressed against the soft flesh alongside the edge of the triangle and felt the moist warmth of her. "Yes, oh, please yes, go on . . . go on . . ." Leah breathed and when he touched the edge of the butter-soft lips and held there, her scream was suddenly piercing. Her hips twisted and pushed upward for his touch and he slid into the warm, moist darkness and her cries gasped out hymns of pleasure.

She had begun with a hint of deliberateness in her lovemaking but it was gone now, absolutely gone. Leah's cries, surgings, wantings, were all unvarnished, no calculation to anything, only the pleasure of wanting and the wanting of pleasure. He touched deeper and her scream answered and he let his fingers probe and caress the soft walls. Leah moaned and he felt her hips twist and lift, her moist thighs closing around him. She raised upward as she cried out, her thighs holding him in the embrace of all embraces and his warm, throbbing organ slid forward slowly. But Leah would have nothing of slowness. With a cry made almost of impatient irritation, she surged forward to take as much of him as possible.

He moved with her, and fell into the rhythm she set. Leah's pale blue eyes remained open, fixed in a stare of almost opaque intensity. "More, more, oh, yes, more," she whispered through lips that quivered, closing, opening and quivering again. Her half gasps, half whispers echoed the surges of her body. She kept her full-fleshed thighs against him, rubbing and pressing, and he felt the delicious softness of her as she surrounded him with her body, thighs, arms, and breasts, every part of her against him, clasping, rubbing, enveloping. Suddenly her long, slow surges grew quicker, an explosion of sudden fervor. "Yes, yes, oh, God . . . now, now, now," she half screamed and she rammed her portal against his groin, her hips lifting upward. He felt the butter-soft walls pressing against his own wanting, and felt himself explode with the frenzied demand she sent him, a sweet, wild message beyond resistance. "Oh God, oh God," Leah gasped out as she pumped against him, her pale white skin suddenly glistening with a covering of tiny beads of perspiration and she lay against him, an almost ghostly wraith of wanting.

Finally, with a sigh that hissed from her, she went limp, the pale white body quivering for a long moment and then growing still. She lay holding his face to her breasts, one tiny, very red tip pressed to his lips. When she let her arms fall to her sides he drew back and met the pale blue eyes that still stared wide open at him. "You do a powerful job of convincing," he said.

"I hope so," Leah said, pushing herself to sit up, her breasts swaying from side to side provocatively. He saw the pale blue eyes search his face questioningly.

"I'd say it was as much enjoying as convincing," Fargo commented.

"I expected that," she said and her eyes continued to search his face.

"We've a deal," he said and her slow smile held an edge of triumph.

"You'll tell Buzz in the morning," Leah said as she reached for her shirt. He nodded and watched her dress. Her arms came around him when she finished. "It'll be even better when you get back," she said.

"That'll be hard to do," he said.

"Trust me," she said.

"What if I don't find the stage?" he questioned.

She shrugged. "I didn't set any conditions, did

I?" Leah said. She stepped from him and started for the door. She glanced back when she opened the door, the pale blue eyes smug. Fargo lay back. Leah had gotten what she wanted. He just wasn't certain exactly what that had been. Keeping silent about having his mind made up already had been the right thing to do, he told himself again, drawing sleep quickly around himself. Some things weren't helped by too much examination.

3

When morning came he breakfasted at the inn, retrieved the Ovaro, and walked the horse up the already bustling main street. Surprise pushed at him as he saw Melanie Carter and others gathered at the stage depot. She stepped forward as he halted. "Good morning. We heard you were at the inn but decided to wait here," she said.

"Got a proposition for you," Rod Harris said. "We heard who you are. We want you to find the passengers who were on that stage, Fargo. We'll pool our funds to pay you."

"Sorry, you're too late," Fargo said. "I'm hired."

"Buzz Collins?" Melanie Carter frowned.

"He wants his stage," Fargo said.

"I want Steven Tinsdale and the documents he was bringing," Rod Harris said.

"I want my cousin, Lucy," Melanie Carter said.

"And I want my brother, Roger," Ralph Abel chimed in.

"You can't do this. You can't put a stagecoach over people," Melanie Carter said sharply. "What kind of man are you?"

"The kind who keeps his word when he gives it," Fargo said.

But Melanie Carter wasn't about to be satisfied.

"Turn it around. First the passengers, then go look for the stage," she said.

"Going after the stage is my best bet. I find the stage, maybe I'll find the passengers," he said. It was not a completely hollow answer, it just wasn't one he could believe in.

"Maybe's not good enough for me," Rod Harris said.

"Nor for me," Melanie snapped.

"It's the best I can do," Fargo said.

"I won't stand still for that," Melanie said, her brown eyes flashing dark fire.

"You don't have any choice, honey," he said. He didn't want to be cruel but he hadn't the time to argue. Besides, she was thorny, the kind who didn't give up easily. It was in the determined set of her pretty face. He moved the pinto forward and saw the hurt in Winifred Bivins's face as she clutched the little girl and for a moment he wished he hadn't made the commitment to Leah. But he had and finding the stage was still the best bet. He rode on to the end of town where Leah opened the door for him as he dismounted. His little smile was made of the unsaid and Buzz Collins strode from the adjoining room.

"Just came from the bank," Collins said.

"It's a deal," Fargo said and wondered why the stab of discomfort went through him. Perhaps it was the pleading in Winifred Bivins's eyes, he told himself as he pocketed the bills Buzz Collins gave him. "A couple of things might help," he said to Collins. "All four stages full Concords?"

"That's right, from Abbot and Downing," Buzz Collins said.

"Then they'd each have a coachmaker's mark and number," Fargo said. "I don't want to be chasing down a wrong stage."

Collins disappeared into the next room to return with four sheets of paper. "Take these," he said and Fargo looked at the four bills of sale. Each bore the company's name across the top: ABBOT & DOWNING, COACHMAKERS—CONCORD, MASSACHUSETTS. He read the coach numbers at the bottom of each sheet—coach 1290, coach 1351, coach 1400, coach 1433, and pushed the papers into his pocket. "You find my stages. I'll go bring them back," Buzz Collins said.

"I'll do my best," Fargo said.

"That's what I'm counting on," Collins said and left the room. Leah walked outside with Fargo, halting beside the Ovaro with him.

"You counting on anything?" he asked her.

"Your remembering last night," she said.

"Hell, that's not hard to count on," he said and her kiss was quick, almost perfunctory, and she was back in the house before he'd ridden from the yard. He went back through Bolton Flats. It was the most direct route and he slowed down when he reached the stage depot. But there was no one there. They'd given up on more demands and futile waiting. Sometimes commonsense won out, he thought as he made his way from the town. Under the noon sun he began to retrace his steps. At the first set of hills, the sun had moved into afternoon. When he reached the second set of rocks where he had first seen the runaway stage, the sun was lining the distant peaks. Pushing the Ovaro harder, he managed to reach the spot where the tracks of the stage had simply vanished. The sun was moving down behind the peaks and night was beginning to roll in as he rode into the softer land that bordered the rocky road. He found a stand of red ash and dismounted.

Unsaddling the Ovaro, he let the horse graze in a cluster of bluegrass and set out his bedroll. He made a note to find a place to replenish his supply of jerky and dried beef strips. Shooting fresh game was both a luxury and a chore he didn't want to take on. The night rolled over the land and he felt the tiredness in his body. It had been an intense ride back and he lay down and shed his clothes on the bedroll as he chewed on the dried beef. Thoughts idly drifted through his mind as he finished eating and he lay on the edge of sleep. The question that slid over him made him again aware of the uneasiness that still clung to him. Why was Buzz Collins paying the kind of money that'd buy him four brand-new stages? That still made no sense. It wasn't sentimental attachment. Collins didn't know the word *sentiment.* A matter of principle? Fargo grimaced. That wasn't a word Collins was terribly familiar with, either, he was certain.

What then? The question nagged at him. Was the reason he so desperately wanted the four stages back connected with why they had been stolen in the first place? The thought tantalized him. But Collins had been honestly at a loss to explain the disappearance of the stages. If there was a connection, he hadn't made it. Fargo put the question away in a corner of his mind to perhaps visit again. He closed his eyes and let sleep begin its embrace. A new moon began to climb its way across the blue velvet sky and he was almost asleep when his eyes snapped open.

It was the Ovaro that had yanked him awake. The horse was suddenly alert, moving its feet in place. Fargo sat up, his hand closing around the butt of the Colt in the holster that lay at his side. He saw the Ovaro's ears standing up straight as they twitched. He heard the sound, then a horse blowing air, a soft snort. Some hundred yards away, Fargo guessed. He waited and after a few minutes the horse gave another snort. From the same distance, Fargo noted. It hadn't moved closer. He rose and strapped on his gunbelt. Staying on foot, he moved forward at a crouch. Maybe someone had just bedded down nearby, but he immediately frowned at the thought. This wasn't an area anyone would pick to travel through. He hadn't expected to be followed; he hadn't paid any attention to the possibility.

But by now there'd been plenty of time for talk about his looking for the stages. Gossip was like the wind. It traveled fast in all directions. Perhaps he had been followed. Anything was possible. He moved forward on the balls of his feet. The terrain stayed flat, but he was glad for the tall brush, mostly broomsedge and vervain, that provided good enough cover. He paused and listened. The horse blew air through his nostrils again and changed direction. He had gone at least fifty yards, slowly and carefully, when he picked up the tiny flicker of light. The light became a small flame, not more than a few twigs barely burning. A figure lay curled up asleep beside the tiny fire, a hat pulled over its face, legs drawn up.

Fargo moved closer, the Colt in his hand now. Halting a few feet from the burning twigs, he leveled the pistol at the sleeping figure. "You've got company, mister," he said. The figure woke, startled, whirled, and sat up, the hat falling to the ground. Fargo stared at the round-cheeked face, the small nose and brown hair. "Jesus, you," he bit out. Melanie Carter stared back, her eyes still wide, startled. But she swallowed hard and her chin tilted upward defiantly.

"You always sneak up on people when they're asleep?" she tossed back.

"When I think they've been following me," Fargo said, holstering the Colt. "That's what you were doing, weren't you?"

Her lips tightened but the defiance stayed in her face. "I couldn't see your tracks after it got dark," she said. "I decided to sleep and go on in the morning."

"You don't build a fire when you're trailing somebody," he said.

"It got cold out here. It was only a little fire. I didn't know I was this close to you," Melanie said.

"Get up, bring your horse," he said and started to walk back to where he had his things. She followed and caught up to him as he reached the Ovaro. He pulled a blanket from his saddlebag and tossed it to her. "Use this till you go back come morning," he said gruffly.

"I'm not going back in the morning," she muttered.

"You're not following me," Fargo said.

"Dammit, why can't you look for the passengers first?" Melanie asked with anger and despair in her voice. "I want to find Lucy. They might be holding her and the others."

He swore inwardly. She was stubborn and determined. Only harsh reality would reach her, he decided. "It seems pretty clear that the stage was hijacked, probably by whoever hijacked the other three. Why, is anybody's guess. Truth is, it's not likely they left any passengers. No witnesses, nobody talks." He gestured to the vastness of the flat, brush-covered land and rock-strewn hills bordering it. "That's an awful lot of land for burying a few passengers," he said.

"And their belongings?" she asked.

"Most likely buried with them. They wouldn't want to leave things around that could be found and start hunts," Fargo said. "Everything could be buried anywhere. I find the stage, I've a chance to find out about the passengers. That's still the best bet."

She fell silent, wrapped in the blanket and her own thoughts. Finally, she lay back and in a little while he heard the steady breathing of sleep coming from her. He put his gunbelt beside his sleeping bag and quickly welcomed his own return to sleep. A rufous-sided towhee woke him in the morning with its distinctive call. He rose up on his elbows, saw Melanie a half-dozen feet from him, sitting up, her eyes on him. He blinked and her hand came into focus. It held a revolver pointed at him, a Joslyn army piece, he saw, five-shot, single-action, a good, accurate gun. "What do you think you're doing?" he asked.

"Making sure I go with you to find that stage,"

she said. "That's what I promised the others I'd do."

"I don't work at the point of a gun," he said.

"This time you'll make an exception," Melanie said. "Push your gunbelt over here." He eyed the Joslyn. It was steady and much too close to miss. He used his foot to push the gunbelt to her. She reached out, pulled the Colt free, and pushed it into her waistband.

"You know how to use that thing?" he said, nodding to the Joslyn she held.

"See the top of that clump of vervain, the tallest one?" she asked with a flick of her eyes. He noted the shrub and the tallest of three stems. The Joslyn barked and he saw the top of the shrub disintegrate in a shower of foliage. He brought his glance back to Melanie.

"Where you'd learn to shoot like that?" he asked.

"My daddy taught me, years ago. He said a girl out in this country ought to know how to shoot," she answered.

"This still won't work, you know," Fargo said. "You going to stay awake all night every night?"

"Yes. You'll be tied up," she said.

"And every time we stop to water the horses or eat?" he pushed at her.

"I'll be careful," she said, keeping her face determined. But he'd caught the moment of apprehension in her voice, fleeting yet nonetheless there. Yet she'd try, he knew. That much was in the defiance of her snub-nosed pretty face. She'd try and slow him down till he got the chance to get to her. He didn't want that. Time was important. He smiled at her and drew a frown.

"You're a real little hard nose, aren't you?" he conceded.

"I have to find Lucy and her things," she said. "All you have to do is agree to take me along."

"We'll play it your way," he said, pushing to his feet and starting for the Ovaro. "There's a pond up a way. Got a glimpse of it just as it was getting dark. We can wash up and water the horses there," he said.

"Ride in front of me and keep away from that rifle," she said. He swung onto the Ovaro after he put away his things. She was waiting in the saddle and he swung in front of her. The little pond was no more than that, near the hills, but filled with fresh, cool water from an underground spring. He'd already made a decision but he'd be damned if he let her think she'd won. Halting at the edge of the pond, he swung to the ground. "I'm going to wash. I'll be gathering enough road grit in the next few days," he said as he dismounted. "You'll have to keep your eyes on me, of course."

"I know what I have to do," she said with annoyance.

"I'll just step behind this rock," he said, moving behind the piece of granite that came to just above his shoulders. He shed his clothes, unstrapped the calf holster with the thin throwing blade from around his leg, and lay it atop his clothes. He made no move to use it. There was no need, he was certain. Stepping naked from behind the rock, he lowered himself into the pool and smiled inwardly as he saw her eyes move across the muscled contours of his body. They stayed on him as he sank into the pond water, dipped under the surface, came up, and turned, letting himself float lazily. Quick glances at her showed that she hadn't taken her eyes from him, but for the wrong reasons, and he smiled again to himself. "I hope you're not enjoying this," he said and saw the dots of color come into her cheeks. "For shame," he said and dived under the surface again. When he came up the color had flooded her cheeks but she kept her lips in a thin line.

He floated to the edge of the pond near her and stayed there lazily, most of his body clearly visible. "I think that's enough. Get out," Melanie said sharply.

"I'm enjoying myself," he protested.

"You're not here to enjoy yourself," she admonished.

"I'm letting you enjoy yourself," he said.

The red in her cheeks deepened. "I'm not enjoying myself," she snapped reproachfully.

"Lying is a sin," he said blandly and let himself float to the shoreline.

"That's enough, dammit," Melanie said and stepped to the edge of the pond. "Get out of there. You've a stagecoach to find."

"You're the boss," he said and stood up, his naked, muscled body glistening with drops of water. He saw her eyes drop to his pelvis, the pistol dipping as they did. His left hand slightly behind him, he slapped downward, hit the pond with a scooping motion. The water struck Melanie in the face. She blinked and yelped, her eyes

43

closed for a split second. But that was enough for Fargo. His right hand shot out, grabbed her ankle and pulled. She went down, the shot going wildly into the air as her finger automatically tightened on the trigger. He was out of the water and on top of her instantly, and twisted the gun from her hand. He stayed half on top of her and pressed his body on hers.

"Damn you," she hissed and glared up at him.

"That's what comes from looking instead of watching," he said.

Her cheeks turned red again. "Damn you," she hissed. He laughed as he pushed up from her, and stepped back and walked behind the rock. He looked out at her from over the top of the rock as he dressed. She sat up and buttoned the top of the green traveling dress where it had come open. When dressed, he came from behind the rock. Her round-cheeked face was a combination of truculence and defiance. "You don't know what you'll be finding. I could help you," she said. "You know I can shoot."

"I won't have time to watch out for anybody but myself," he said.

"Then I'll keep following you. It's a free country." She glowered at him.

He tossed the Joslyn at her. "Put that away and mount up if you're going to come," he said. Her lips fell open and her eyes widened in surprise.

"You're taking me?" she said.

"Decided to before you pulled your little stunt," he said and her frown was instant. "I just wanted to show you you couldn't get away with it," he said.

44

"Damn you," she said.

"You better get something else to say to me," he said and felt the surprise sweep through him as she came forward, flung her arms around him, and pressed full, warm lips to his.

"Thanks," she said when she pulled away. "That better?"

"Much," he said and climbed onto the Ovaro. She took her mount and rode beside him as he scanned the place where the stage tracks had disappeared. Nothing more revealed itself as he searched and he finally let out a soft oath.

"How do you wipe out stage tracks?" Melanie said.

"It takes doing. They were good," Fargo said. "We'll have to check all this land."

"I can take one section. It'll save time," Melanie said.

His smile was rueful. "It would, if you knew how to track," he said.

"Hell, I surely can see wheel tracks," Melanie said.

"Can you?" he asked patiently. "Show me the ones here."

"There aren't any wheel tracks here. You just said so yourself," she snapped.

"I said there weren't any stage tracks," he told her. He waited as she frowned and let her eyes sweep the ground. He motioned for her to dismount with him and she stood at his side as he pushed aside the dark green leaves of a carpet of milk thistle, pressing apart the viny growth until the wheel tracks came into view, faint, shallow, and narrow. "A light buckboard came through here that left a track that didn't crush down the leaves and vines the way a big Concord would have. They were able to spring back up."

"If they sprang back up how'd you know the tracks were there?" Melanie asked.

"They sprang up but not exactly as they had been. The ones that sprang up are pressed together differently from the rest of the field. That's what you look for when you're tracking, the little things that tell you what you don't see right away," he said.

"Jeez," Melanie whispered. "Guess I'm no trailsman."

"You might be before we're finished if you keep your eyes open," he said and climbed back into the saddle. He set a pattern that let him cross and recross his steps as the day wore on. Melanie stayed close and listened to the things he pointed out, but as the day neared an end he found no Concord tracks. "They've been real careful. They could only do it by covering their tracks every half hour," he said.

"Which means they couldn't have made good time," she said.

"Right. Guess we should be grateful for small favors," he said as he halted beside a stand of red ash. "We'll bed down here," he said with an eye to the night sliding over the land. Melanie unsaddled her horse and set out the blanket and he put his bedroll nearby. She was not easy to read, he decided. She had been attentive, eager to listen and learn, but sometimes her full lips almost carried a pout, as though she were unhappy with the ways of things. Yet one thing was clear. Her determination never wavered, never softened the prettiness of her face. It was as though something inside was driving her, something more than wanting to find her cousin.

He peered into the last of the day. The land was becoming all rolling hills with thick, heavy tree cover. Yet he spied plenty of open spaces between the growths of yellow quaking aspen, silver fir, and full, triangular-leafed cottonwoods. She picked up his thoughts with an ease that surprised him. "Is it going to get harder?" she asked.

"Yes, in some ways, no in others," he said.

"Give me a yes," she said. "Lots of heavy tree cover in which to stash a stage?"

"There'd be no reason to stash a stage out here in this wildness. But there's plenty of cover for northern Shoshone and Nez Percé to hide," he said.

"Give me a no," she said.

"There are less places for them to have traveled. I'm going to stick to the open low ground. It's logical they did," he said. His eyes took her in for a long moment. "You have something beside that traveling dress?" he asked. "It's not exactly a riding outfit."

"Yes," she said as night fell. She went behind the trees and emerged in a flannel nightgown that hid most of her in its gray folds. He stretched out on his bedroll as they ate cold beef strips and when she finished, she stared into the night, a tiny furrow creasing her brow.

"You're thinking real hard, Melanie Carter," he said.

"I'm beginning to wonder if we'll ever find Lucy and her things," she said.

"You discourage so easily?" he asked.

"No, but I don't like to be a fool, either," she said.

"Why is it so important that you find her things?" Fargo queried.

"She was bringing family papers, documents that are important to me," Melanie answered.

"Seems everybody on that stage was bringing something," Fargo remarked.

"Guess so," she said and lay back, cutting off the conversation. "Good night," she said.

"I was hoping for maybe a good night kiss," he slid at her.

"I said my thank you. Don't make any more of it," she said with flat reproach in her tone.

"Wouldn't think of it. You might use that Joslyn again," he laughed teasingly.

"I might," she said, no amusement in her voice. He lay back, closed his eyes, and slept quickly, waking once to the soft sound of deer nearby and the chatter of foxes in the distance. When he woke with the morning, he sat up to see Melanie buttoning a dark red shirt that hung lightly on the curve of modest but high breasts. Blue jeans encased her legs tightly and he noted a firm, very round, compact little rear, as sassy in its own way as her snub-nosed, determined face. He washed with water from his canteen, found a cluster of wild plum for breakfast, and as the sun began to warm the morning he got on the Ovaro and rode west. He headed into a wide swath of land that led downward at a gentle slope well covered with the deep yellow of alpine sunflower and the bright red of strawberry leaves. He searched the swath between the rows of aspen and found no sign of any wheel marks.

But he did come upon a fast-running stream, deep enough to bathe in as it leaped over flat rocks. Its speed was evidence that it coursed down from high in the hills and Melanie swung from her horse. "My turn," she said. He shrugged, swung to the ground, and leaned against the dark, rough bark of an old aspen. "You just going to stand there?" She frowned.

"Why not? You did," he said blandly.

"That was different," she said.

"You want me to hold a Colt on you? Will that make it all right?" he asked.

"I want you to be a gentleman," she said. "I *had* to watch you. It's not the same."

He tossed her a smile. "I'm feeling kindly," he said and sauntered away down the slope. He halted at a spot that let him look out across the hills to the towering, distant peaks of the Bitterroot Range. This was a land men were trying to tame, to build footholds in, and this was a land that fought back and refused the taming of men with every weapon nature offered. He wanted to find the stage before he had to go further into that land. It held far too many ways to put a sudden end to his search.

Yet the stage seemed to have thoroughly vanished, as if by magic. But magic was for the Shoshone shamans and the hidden ways of the wild creatures. The men who'd left him for dead were hijackers, not high priests. They had made the stage disappear by guile and cleverness, not magic. They had left clues, someplace, somewhere, dammit. They always did. Finally, he turned and strolled up the slope to find Melanie with her jeans on, reaching for her blouse. Her back was to him, a nice back, strong, smooth and firm, he noted, pronounced shoulder blades and wide shoulders. She heard him and slipped the blouse on before turning around. Her skin wasn't completely dry and he saw the little twin points that clung to the blouse, beautifully high and erect.

"Let's ride," he said and she swung onto her horse with a tiny smile touching her full lips, a hint of smugness in it. She stayed beside him as he moved down the swatch of open land. He kept the pinto at a walk as he scanned every inch of the terrain, peering into the aspen on both sides. But the land refused to reveal anything and he continued down the slope.

"Maybe we're looking in the wrong place," Melanie offered, dismay coming into her voice.

"No. They wouldn't be climbing the hills with a stage. They've just been very thorough," he said with grudging admiration. The slope began to level off somewhat in its downward path and the swath of open land narrowed. They had begun to move into the midafternoon and he had to force himself to keep to the slow, painstaking pace. But he did so, refusing to let frustration push him into carelessness. The first break came soon after and he almost missed it as the path made a slow curve. But his probing eyes caught the object, a darker shape inside the edge of the trees, and he pulled the Ovaro to a halt and dropped from the saddle. He plunged into the edge of the aspen, scooped up the object, and emerged holding it in his hand. "Bull's-eye," he said. "I almost missed it."

"It looks like some kind of broom," Melanie said.

"It is, a splint broom," he said. "You don't see many of them anymore. The broom part's made of very thin, flexible wood splints that are just stiff enough to make them perfect for brushing away tracks in the dirt. I'm sure they have a number of them. They left this one behind. Their first mistake."

"But that wouldn't cover up tracks in grass and brush," Melanie said.

"No. They used other things for that, whatever they are," Fargo said and climbed into the saddle. Moving on down the slope, he continued to search into the trees but found nothing else. But he didn't really expect to. They had been very careful. But the splint broom was enough, all he needed to know they were on the right track. The day was beginning to fade away when the slope leveled off entirely, and widened again. As they rounded a slow curve, the river appeared in front of them.

Melanie's surprise echoed his own and drawing closer, he saw that the river was wide and flowed rapidly on a strong current. Moving along the bank, he saw the house a dozen feet from the river. It was small and made of half rough-hewn logs and uneven stones. A large shed stood to the right of the house but it was the wood plank landing at the shore that drew his eyes. A huge, flat raft was moored to the landing and Fargo read the crudely lettered sign alongside it:

RAFT FOR HIRE
MIKE HORGAN

He glanced at Melanie as she too took in the size of the raft. "What are you thinking?" she whispered.

"I'm wondering a lot of things," he said as the door of the house opened and a man in trousers and an undershirt stepped outside. "You Mike Horgan?" Fargo asked and took in a wiry build with long muscles, an equally long face, and wary eyes.

"That's right. What can I do for you?" the man said.

"Never saw a raft this big," Fargo said with a glance at the raft. "Especially made?"

"That's right," the man said.

"What do you carry on it?" Fargo inquired casually.

"Furniture, household goods, crates, and barrels," Horgan said.

"You could carry a stage and team on that raft," Fargo said pleasantly and saw the man's jaw drop open. "Ever do that?"

"No. No, what made you say that?" Horgan frowned, his eyes moving nervously.

"Just a thought," Fargo said. Mike Horgan licked his lips nervously. "What's this river?" Fargo queried.

"It's an offshoot of the Salmon."

"It go all the way into Idaho Territory?" Fargo asked.

"Yep."

"We were thinking of heading into Idaho," Fargo said with a glance at Melanie. "A raft would make it much easier than riding."

"Not this raft. It's much too big for just the two of you," Horgan said quickly.

"Plenty of room. I like that," Fargo said, glancing admiringly at the raft.

"It's too big for one man to pole. I've two helpers on it. That makes it too expensive for anything but big loads," Horgan said doggedly.

"It's for hire, isn't it?" Fargo said, turning aggressive. "You've got a sign that says so."

"Yes, it's for hire," Horgan said, but with distinct unhappiness.

"Then it's settled. We're hiring the raft. Have your helpers ready to go come morning," Fargo said, letting annoyance and determination color his tone. The man nodded sullenly and Fargo beckoned for Melanie to follow as he rode away. He retraced his steps in the darkness until he turned and pushed the Ovaro into the forest of aspen and swung from the saddle. "We're onto something. Mr. Horgan's much too unhappy," he whispered.

"You think he's part of it?" Melanie asked.

"Maybe he's only hired help but he knows what's going on," Fargo said.

"What now?" Melanie questioned.

"I'm betting he's going off someplace for instructions," Fargo said as he tethered the horses to a branch and started through the trees on foot.

"Taking the stage by raft is a perfect solution. No tracks to worry about once they get it here. Let's find out if I'm right," he said. Melanie stayed at his heels as he made his way back through the trees to the river. He came in sight of the house just as the door opened and Horgan came out, a kerosene lamp in one hand. He went behind the house, returned soon after with a small, gray mare. Setting the lamp on the ground, he climbed onto the mare and rode northwest along the riverbank.

Fargo's trailsman's ears listened and caught the change in the sound of the hoofbeats as the horse left the riverbank and went inland. He waited till the hoofbeats faded away before stepping from the trees. Melanie beside him, he picked up the lamp and went to the shed, pulled the door open, and let the lamp illuminate the interior. The first item he saw was a stack of a dozen more splint brooms and then his eyes went to the equipment on the floor. "Bull's-eye, again," Fargo said. "Look here, long-handled scythes, smaller, one-hand reaping sickles, wooden threshing flails and plenty of rakes. This is it. This is what they used to smooth out tracks in grass, high brush and weeds, the places the splint brooms couldn't touch. They used the scythes and reaping sickles to cut away the tracks, the threshing flails to cover up whatever the scythes didn't get. With the rakes they pulled away what they'd cut and smoothed. No wonder there wasn't a damn trail left anywhere," Fargo said.

"They brought the stage here and shipped it the

rest of the way by raft. We've got that much nailed down," Melanie said.

"Now we have to see where the rest of this trail takes us," Fargo said. Closing the shed door, he put the lamp back where Horgan had placed it.

"We going to wait for him to get back?" Melanie asked.

"No, that won't tell us anything. Tomorrow will, I'm betting," he said and Melanie walked with him back into the aspen. Retrieving the horses, he put some more distance between them and the river and settled into a thicket deep in the trees. The moon filtered in enough light for him to see Melanie change behind a wide-trunked aspen. She returned in the flannel nightgown and sat beside him on the blanket. They ate quickly, in silence, and when they were finished, he saw her round-cheeked face grow tight again.

"All this doesn't tell us anything about the prisoners," she said.

"Don't expect we'll know that till we find the stage," Fargo said.

Her hand came out, closed over his. He pushed up on his elbows and peered at her as she sat cross-legged, wrapped in the nightgown. "Thanks for getting us here," Melanie said. "I understand why Buzz Collins was so eager to pay you to find his stages."

"I'm not sure I do," Fargo said, thinking about pay that was more than the stages were worth.

"What's that mean?" Melanie frowned.

"Nothing. Just some unfinished questions," Fargo said, unwilling to go into the matter further.

"I don't think anyone else would have gotten us this far," she said.

"There's no telling what's going to come along from here on. You want to cut out now if you like? You could go back to Bolton's Flats and wait," he told her.

"No, absolutely not," she said, no hesitation in her answer. "Finding Lucy, helping you find the stage, it's all tied up together for me now."

"Your call," Fargo said and she nodded. Her hand stayed over his, he noted, as she fell asleep.

4

Morning brought a warm sun and dark thoughts. Fargo rose slowly, making no effort to hurry. He'd be playing a tricky and probably dangerous game but it was one he had to play. Neither time nor opportunity allowed him to do anything different. A trickle of a stream was enough to let him wash and he saddled the horses as Melanie took her turn. A flash of bare skin came through the trees as she bathed, rose, and dried herself, enough only to let him glimpse the sturdy compactness of her. Dressed, she came to him as he finished tightening a cinch. "Keep that Joslyn where you can get to it fast," he said as they set off for the river.

"It's in my skirt pocket," Melanie said. "You expect there'll be trouble."

"Sooner or later," he said. When they reached the river and the landing, Horgan was beside the big raft, two men standing atop it, each holding a long pole.

"Howie and Eddie," Horgan said with a gesture to the two men. Both kept their hard faces expressionless, their nods perfunctory, though Fargo saw Howie linger on Melanie a fraction of a minute longer. "Walk your horses on," Horgan said and Fargo dismounted. He led the Ovaro onto the raft,

Melanie following. Neither horse was happy on the raft, the swaying motion instantly unsettling.

"Keep hold of your reins," he said to Melanie and helped her keep her horse in hand. "Stroke him. Stay close to him. He'll calm down," Fargo told her and turned to Horgan. "Take the river all the way," he said. "What's your next main stop?"

"Elkton, all the way into Idaho," Horgan said.

"How long?" Fargo questioned.

"Two days at best, usually three. Depends on how fast the river's running," Horgan said. "We put in anywhere we can overnight."

"Any bad spots?"

"Too many," Horgan said sourly as he cast off the mooring line and pushed the raft away from the landing. The strong current seized the raft at once, sending it into midriver. Horgan picked up his own pole and joined Howie and Eddie in poling the raft into a straight course. They used the long poles to push and stem the water's flow; they acted as rudders to guide the raft across the top of the river. They worked hard, he saw, the river picking up speed almost at once.

Fargo's eyes went to the shores as the river ran through country dense with thick growths of cottonwoods, hackberry, box elder, and silver fir. He watched the towering peaks of the distant Bitterroot and Lost Beaver ranges where Douglas fir and lodgepole pine dominated the mountains. Both horses had calmed down and he was able to search the shores as the raft made its way downriver. He saw plenty of game, elk, grizzly, whitetails, the ubiquitous beaver and raccoon. Grouse took wing from the shoreline in explosions of short, upward flight whenever the raft drew near. Horgan and the other two men were kept busy handling the raft, Fargo saw with satisfaction as he watched them move back and forth with their long poles. They were good at their work, he saw. When the river entered a strangely calm spot, Horgan came closer to where Fargo rested near the raft's edge.

"You figure to get off at Elkton?" the man asked.

"We might. Depends on what we see there," Fargo said.

"It's a good town, a place where folks stop to get ready to go on west and north," Horgan said. "Of course, there's a lot of work to be done hacking trails across the mountains." He bent to his pole and Fargo continued to scan the shore on both sides as the day wore on. He moved closer to Melanie as she stood at the edge of the raft.

"Seems pretty calm," she murmured. "Maybe they're not really involved."

"Too calm," Fargo said, sweeping the shore with a long glance.

"You expect an attack from shore?" Melanie asked.

"It'd be the best bet," Fargo said.

"With rowboats?"

"No. This current's too fast. I'd guess a heavy barrage of gunfire," Fargo said.

"There's no place to take cover," Melanie said, glancing around the raft.

"Anything happens, you drop flat and stay there," Fargo said.

"What about Horgan and the other two?" she asked.

"I'll have them covered the minute I hear a shot," Fargo said and moved from her to the other side of the raft for a closer look at the shore, where a heavy cluster of peach leaf willow hung over the bank. But nothing happened as the raft sailed by and the day wore on. Fargo felt the furrow sliding across his forehead. Nothing at all had happened and he was both grateful and uneasy for that. The shadows of dusk began to close over the river and the towering mountains that rose up on both sides of it. Were they being watched from onshore, he wondered. Were watchers waiting for them to put into shore for the night before attacking? Melanie had moved to the stern edge of the raft, he saw, and the raftman called Howie was poling only a few feet from her.

The shadows lengthened when suddenly the raft spurted forward. Fargo's eyes went to the river and saw the swirls and frothy ripples erupt. Howie and Eddie were poling hard and he shot a glance at Horgan as the raft gathered speed. "Whitewater?" he shouted.

"Close to it. This is a bad passage," Horgan answered. Fargo felt the raft swing wildly, almost turn sideways, then swing back again. The river drove it forward, turning it despite the efforts of the raftmen. Fargo saw whitewater appear, spitting and hissing with rip currents, reveling in its power. Fargo's eyes sought Melanie. She was still at the rear edge of the raft, Eddie almost beside her as he drew his pole from the water. The shore rushed past, suddenly further away as the raft spun again and he bent his legs to steady himself. The scream came, piercing the air, Melanie's voice a sharp, abrupt cry.

Fargo whirled, just in time to see her going over the side of the raft. Eddie was there, his arms still raised as he finished pushing her. Fargo shouted a curse and the man spun and yanked at his gun. Fargo's draw was a flash of lightning and Eddie did a half spin as two shots slammed into him. He toppled over and lay still on the raft in an instant stain of red. Fargo's eyes went to Horgan and Howie. Both waited, hands poised, but neither was stupid enough to draw. However Horgan's smiling snarl said everything. Fargo could take the time to shoot it out with them but each split second brought Melanie closer to death. The bastards had been more clever than he'd expected. They'd planned it that way, given him a devil's choice with his own death waiting in the wings.

He cursed as he holstered the Colt and dived headlong from the raft into the churning whitewater. It had already swept Melanie away, he knew, and he hit the water knowing only luck would find her. As he surfaced, he heard the loud splash and turned to see that the Ovaro had leaped from the raft. The horse swam toward him, its power letting it push through the surging water as he never could. He swam toward it as the raft was swept downriver. Horgan kept on firing all of his shots wild and wide of their target. As the rafter all but disappeared from view, the Ovaro reached him and Fargo managed to grab hold of a stirrup and pull himself closer to the horse as the Ovaro fought the pull of the whitewater.

Getting hold of the saddle horn, Fargo swam alongside the horse as he scanned the leaping, hissing water and cursed at how quickly dusk swept down on the river. Desperation pulling at him, he swam downriver beside the horse, clinging gratefully to its strength as his eyes swept the water. The river reached a wide curve when he glimpsed the dark bulk tossed upward on a rush of white-crested water. An arm flailed upward and Fargo pulled at the horse, turning it toward Melanie's form. The Ovaro responded, its weight and power propelling it through the water and Fargo along with it. As the horse closed the distance to where the river spun Melanie in a circle, Fargo let go of his hold on the saddle and struck out for Melanie's turning, twisting body.

He reached her and closed both arms around her and struck out for the shore. Suddenly and capriciously, the river decided to help and he felt himself being carried upward on a surge of water and swept toward the shoreline. Clinging to Melanie, he went with the rush of crosscurrent. His feet soon were touching bottom sand. He struggled for better footing, found it, and pulled himself forward. Melanie a limp weight in his grasp, he fell, kept his grip on her, and pushed himself upward as he staggered up the soft earth of the shore. He realized his strength and his breath were almost at an end as he reached a dry part of the bank. He managed to find the power for a last, desperate effort and collapsed onto dry earth.

He lay, gasping in air, his arms still clutching Melanie. He finally pushed upward to set Melanie facedown on her stomach. He heard his own gasped cry of relief as he felt her body shake, then he heard the gargling sound come from her, a rush of air and water being expelled from her lungs. She lay heaving, gasping, and throwing up more water and he thought he had never heard so welcome a sound. Finally she lay breathing in long drafts of air. Not looking up, she reached out, curled a hand around his arm, and lay there as the dusk turned to night.

Fargo looked up and saw the Ovaro pulling itself from the water a dozen yards downriver. The horse paused, shook itself, and came toward him. Fargo pushed to his feet, pulled the saddlebag open, and took out towels and his sleeping bag. Melanie was sitting up as he returned to her and threw one of the towels to her. She clung to him wordlessly, her body trembling. Only partly from the wetness, he knew. "Get those clothes off and get dry," he said and began pulling off his own soaked garments. As Melanie used the towels, he hung his clothes and hers on the low branches of a hackberry and pulled the sleeping bag open. "Get in and get warm," he said, drying himself. She crawled in, a soft white blur in the blackness of the new night and he slid in beside her. In moments, they were enveloped in the warmth of their own body heat and he felt Melanie pressed close against him, her breasts very soft, pushing flat into his chest, her legs half around his.

She stayed there, not moving. "I thought I was finished," she murmured. "I managed to get quick breaths of air as I was tossed upward."

"They thought they could get to me through

you. It almost worked. They were clever," Fargo said.

"Where are they now?" Melanie asked.

"Downriver someplace. They won't be able to pull to shore until they're past the whitewater. That'll be a ways down, I'd guess. This whitewater's moving too fast to drop away quickly. They'll eventually put in for the night somewhere."

Melanie stayed against him and it wasn't long before the sleeping bag grew hot and he pulled it open. The night had stayed warm, a soft wind sweeping over them. The moon had come up enough for its pale light to bathe the land and he looked at Melanie as she lay beside him; her breasts were less modest than he'd thought, very beautifully round and full, each tip darkly pink. Broad, strong shoulders combined with a deep rib cage to give her a firm roundness. He took in a compact body, everything about her softly curved, no sharp angles, no long leanness anywhere. A rounded, convex little belly moved down to a pert little triangle, thick and puffy with its own sauciness. She watched his eyes enjoying her young, firm loveliness and she half turned and lifted her arms to encircle his neck.

"We don't know why things happen as they do but they do. It's not right to turn your back on them," she said.

"Not right at all," he agreed and felt her soft, full lips on his, pressing gently, then harder. Her tongue moved forward, slowly, savoring, circling, and she gave a tiny cry as his hand curled around one round, full breast. "Oh yes, yes," Melanie said as she turned to press more of her breast into his palm. His lips left hers and traced an invisible line down her throat, found the dark pink tip of one round breast, and closed around it. Melanie gave a half scream of delight, quivered, and let a low moan escape her as his mouth pulled in the soft mound, sucked on it, caressed the tip with his tongue, and felt it rise in answer.

Melanie's hands moved up and down his body in soft pressing motions, as if she were trying to let touch take in his essence. He caressed the breast and curled one hand around it as he moved his lips away, nibbling a path down across the convex little mound of her belly. "Oh God, oh yes, oh God yes," Melanie gasped as his hand moved into the puffy little triangle and pressed down upon the Venus mound. He let his fingers linger in the thick puffy denseness, her nap a surprisingly soft, flocculent down.

When his hand moved down further and touched the pliant softness of the tiny fold just over the dark portal, Melanie screamed, a sound made of anticipation. He moved his hand into the space between her thighs, which were still held together; he felt the warm moisture of the inside of her thighs, paused, and with a sudden gesture, a kind of abandon, Melanie flung her legs open. "Yes, dammit, oh Jesus, yes," she screamed and her thighs came together again with a slapping sound, holding his hand in a warm, soft vise until she released him again with an upward surge of her torso. He found the wet tip of the sweet lips and caressed it. Melanie's hips lifted and her hand came to his, pressing as she made urgent little sounds. He let himself touch deeper and her hand fell away and came against his leg. She screamed again and pulled at him as she twisted her pelvis.

He brought himself over her and let his searching organ find its home. He thrust forward slowly, Melanie's cry a burst of wanting spiraling into the night. She rose with him, joined with his every thrusting delight, her compact body a sudden explosion of desire. "Yes, yes, yes, yes, yes, yes . . . ii-iiiieeeee," Melanie screamed, wrapped in ecstasy, the body supreme, the senses indulged to their fullest. He went with her and felt the sweet caress of her inner contractions, the warm flowing of her, the wine of wines, nectar of nectars. He buried his face into the very round breasts, reveling in the soft warmth that smothered him with pleasure. Then, in that timeless moment that always came too soon, he felt her body quicken and heard her cry arch into the night. "Oh, God, now, now . . . nooooow," Melanie wailed and he exploded with her as the world spun away.

She kept her legs around him, his face into her breasts after the stars stopped bursting and her wail died away to a reluctant whimper. Finally, her legs fell open, her sweet vise releasing him and he lay beside her, one leg half over her downy little nap. He watched her eyes return to the world and peer at him as a tiny smile crossed her full lips. "I surprised you," she said.

"Guess so. Didn't figure you to be this eager, this explosive," he admitted.

"I learned something a good while ago. When there's something you have to do or want to do, you just do it. No questioning, no searching, no regretting. You just do it," she said.

"What was this, wanting to do or having to do?" He smiled.

"Sometimes wanting is so strong it becomes having," she said and pulled him against her. He listened to her fall asleep and let himself embrace slumber with her. She had surprised him, indeed. But it was the kind of surprise he liked. He slept soundly, putting aside tomorrow until the new day finally dawned.

He awoke with the firm, youthful loveliness of her beside him. She awoke only after he'd left the sleeping bag, washed at the river's edge, and returned. The whitewater still churned, he saw as he watched Melanie at the river. He tossed her a towel as she returned and dressed. "We wait for them to come back looking for us?" she asked.

"No. They think we're done in. They might not come right back. They've got your horse. They might go on to sell him someplace. We'll do the looking," Fargo said. He climbed onto the Ovaro and had Melanie sit in back of him this time. He stayed near the river but inside the trees. The whitewater went on for another few miles. It ended when the river widened, the water quieting down though the current remained strong. They rounded a curve soon after and Fargo reined up, swearing at what he had hoped not to see, the raft moored on the opposite shore. He grimaced and saw Horgan and Howie beside the raft, their long poles in hand.

Melanie's horse was tethered to a white fir nearby and Melanie slid from the saddle with him as Fargo dismounted and drew the rifle from its saddle case. "I could take them both down but I want answers from Horgan," Fargo muttered to Melanie. He dropped to one knee and brought the rifle to his shoulder. Howie put down his pole and began to walk to Melanie's horse as Fargo took aim. He held his shot for another moment, checked out Horgan's position, saw him near the man near the edge of the raft. He brought his eyes back to Howie, lowered the rifle a half inch, and pressed the trigger. The big Henry barked and Howie screamed in pain as he fell clutching at his shattered ankle. "Jesus, oh, Jesus," Howie cried out as he fell to the ground. Horgan whirled and drew his gun, surprise flooding his face as Howie rolled on the ground, his right leg pulled up.

"Drop it or you're dead," Fargo called from inside the trees. Horgan peered across the river, angry realization replacing the surprise on his face. "You've got three seconds," Fargo called. Horgan hesitated, but only for one second before he dropped his gun. "Take Howie's gun and throw it in the river," Fargo ordered. The man walked to where Howie moaned on the ground. Fargo waited and watched Horgan draw Howie's gun and send it into the river in a short arc. "We're coming over. Don't do anything stupid," Fargo said and pulled himself onto the Ovaro. He gestured and Melanie climbed into the saddle behind him. He kept the rifle aimed as he sent the Ovaro from the trees and into the river.

The horse used his power to negotiate across the strong current but Fargo never took his eyes from Horgan, the rifle steady as a rock. "Jesus, help me," Howie was pleading as the Ovaro pulled from the river and climbed the short slope that ran from the edge of the water.

"Stay in the saddle," Fargo muttered to Melanie as he handed her the rifle and dropped to the ground. He walked toward Horgan as Howie looked up.

"Son of a bitch. Get me a doctor," Howie demanded.

"Maybe after your friend here answers some questions," Fargo said, his eyes on Horgan.

"I don't know anything," Horgan blustered.

"I get very angry when people try to bullshit me," Fargo said.

"They just hire me," Horgan said.

"You tried to kill us. Somebody gave you orders," Fargo said. Horgan glowered back tight-lipped. "Talk or it's payback time and I won't think twice about a worthless piece of shit like you," Fargo said. "They brought the stage here. You took it on the raft. Where to?"

"Elkton," Horgan said. Fargo shot a glance at Howie. The man was still holding his shattered ankle, his leg drawn up.

"Who's in Elkton?" Fargo asked, returning his eyes to Horgan.

"Harry Dockerby," Horgan muttered.

"Why? What's this all about?" Fargo pressed.

"I don't know. I just raft the stages to him," Horgan said.

"You've rafted the others, too," Fargo said and the man nodded. Fargo frowned at Horgan and wondered how much more the man really knew. He had let his glances at Howie fall off when he heard the sudden cry, Melanie's voice, then the deep roar of the rifle filling the air. He threw a glance at Howie to see his body jerking spasmodically as a pistol fell from his hand. The sudden sound came from his right and Fargo spun. Horgan was diving for the gun on the ground. "Leave it," Fargo shouted as his hand went to the Colt at his hip.

But Horgan had reached the gun. He flung himself around it as he scooped it up. His shot was too quick and went wild. He never got off another one as the Colt barked, two shots that sounded as one. Horgan's body seemed to skitter backward as it spurted red, shuddered, and lay still. "Goddamn fools, both of them," Fargo spit out.

"The other one had another gun inside his shirt-waist," Melanie said. "I'd no time to do anything but fire when I saw him bring it out."

"You did well," Fargo said. "Get your horse and bring him aboard the raft. We're going to go all the way to Elkton and see what we find out there."

"Can we do it, just the two of us?" Melanie asked.

"We're sure going to try. It'll depend on what the river has in store for us," he said. He led the Ovaro onto the raft and helped Melanie get her horse aboard. When the horses were calmed, he handed her one of the long poles. "Madam raftman," he said and cast off the mooring line that had been tied to a tree. The raft moved from the shore at once, the current instantly seizing it.

Fargo took his pole to the front of the raft while Melanie took up a position at the stern. It took a while and lots of wasted motion and misplaced effort but little by little they got the hang of it, which consisted mostly of using the poles as current breakers to keep the raft on a straight course. Soon Fargo found himself able to scan the shoreline as they moved on down the river, which had become more winding as it cut through mountains that grew ever taller. Flights of grouse continued to wing skyward in their abrupt, almost vertical takeoffs. When the day began to draw to an end, Fargo found a flat place on the riverbank to beach the raft. "Moor it to a tree," he told Melanie. "We're going to have us a proper meal for dinner."

The big Henry in hand, he moved into the lush forest of red ash and white fir. It only took minutes for a covey of grouse to take wing. His first shot missed, his second one didn't, and he returned with a big, fat bird in hand. Melanie had already set out the sleeping bag against the edge of the trees and she began to pluck the grouse as Fargo gathered wood for a campfire. He fashioned a crude spit from an ash branch, and by nightfall the grouse was being roasted. The hot, sweet taste of it was a welcome change and the moon was high when they finished the meal. Fargo put out the fire and after unsaddling the horses, he found Melanie waiting in the sleeping bag for him.

Her arms came around him at once, her firm, young, compact body warm against him. "Aren't you glad you agreed to bring me along?" she asked, smugness in her voice.

"Yes, I am," he admitted honestly. "For all kinds of reasons." She laughed and the night was soon echoing to her cries of delight. Finally she lay satiated beside him and he found one thought hanging in his mind. Melanie made love the same way she pursued finding her cousin and the other passengers, with a total and complete dedication to the goal, whether it was passion or duty. A most unusual young woman, he murmured inwardly, but that was a conclusion he had already come to.

5

They continued downriver in the morning, the surrounding land growing more ruggedly beautiful. "This is Idaho land. I'd guess those are the Sapphire Mountains to the north," Fargo said.

"Which means we could be in Elkton soon," Melanie said.

"Facing Harry Dockerby. We have to have our story ready," Fargo said.

"But what? We don't know anything about him except that Horgan mentioned his name."

"That's enough. We can take a stab at the rest. Somebody's been stealing stagecoaches. Why?"

"To sell them," Melanie said.

"Exactly, and I'm betting Harry Dockerby is our boy. He's selling big Concords he didn't have to buy. His only cost is paying a handful of drifters who don't mind killing innocent people. He's turning a damn handsome profit on each coach," Fargo said.

"If it is this man Dockerby and we find the stages, how do we get them back to Buzz Collins?" Melanie questioned.

"We don't. Collins will come get them. But we have to have a story for Dockerby, one that'll keep him on the hook. I've been working on one. You'll be playing a main role," Fargo said.

"Anything that'll let me find Lucy," she said. Fargo felt reassured by the way she listened, intently absorbing everything he said, and then going over it all again with him. It was midafternoon when they finished polishing everything and Fargo saw the shoreline growing flatter and the very high mountains pulled back from the river. A few cabins came into sight, then back still further from the shore a scattering of houses and cattle. The river narrowed and Fargo pointed to the open area of land as they approached it, a stretch of shoreline where two wooden landings were built out from it.

Behind the landings the clutter of a town rose, mostly wood and clapboard structures, and Fargo pointed to a sign that rose some hundred feet from the landings. ELKTON, it read in crudely painted letters. "Keep poling," he said as the raft came abreast of the landings. "We don't want to go visiting by raft. Somebody might recognize it and start asking questions." Poling furiously, they sent the big raft speeding past the landings. They stayed in midriver until after a long curve Fargo found a spot to steer to shore some five thousands yards from the town. Tying the raft securely to a tree as Melanie walked the horses ashore, he paused in thought for a moment.

"Think we ought to send it downriver?" Melanie asked, reading the question in his mind.

"I'm wondering," he said.

"We might need it again," she said.

"We might." He grimaced, decided to leave the

raft where it was, and climbed onto the pinto. He stayed to the shoreline back to the landings. Then he turned and rode up into the town. Elkton, he quickly saw, was a hard town, the houses showing only the crudest workmanship, the main street made up of long stretches of storage sheds and warehouses. But there was plenty of traffic on the street, mostly Owensboro mountain wagons, though he saw a number of timber wagons with their distinctive "reach" poles hewed in the forests. In the center of town he came upon a sizable building, neatly painted, bearing the sign ELKTON HOTEL over the door, and looking incongruously well tended. Pausing, he called to a man carrying a basket from the building. "Looking for Harry Dockerby," he said.

"End of town," the man answered without waiting for anything more.

"Obliged," Fargo said and rode on with Melanie beside him. At the end of town they found a collection of long covered sheds, a small house with uncurtained windows, and to one side a long bunkhouse with an adjoining stable. A length of canvas hung on the side of one of the sheds and Fargo read the words painted on it:

HARRY DOCKERBY
STAGECOACHES—HAY WAGONS—BUCKBOARDS

As he dismounted, Fargo turned his eyes to the bunkhouse where some eight or ten men lounged outside. They returned his glance with unsmiling, hard stares. The door of the house opened and a man came out, well dressed in a silk shirt with a cravat under a flowered vest, a big Remington in the holster at his hip. But his face didn't reflect his attire, reflecting only a bull-like, heavy coarseness, his nose wide and flat, thick lips, and heavy jowls. Little eyes glittered like that of a rattlesnake's. He wore black hair slicked down but his body was beefy and thick-shouldered, with heavy arms.

"Harry Dockerby. What can I do for you?" he said with a careful smile. Fargo stayed silent and let Melanie answer.

"I'm Melanie Carter. I heard you sell stage-coaches," she said crisply. "I'm interested in buy-ing four good coaches."

Harry Dockerby's eyebrows rose at once. "Well now, you've come to the right place," he said. "But if you don't mind my asking, why would a pretty young lady like you want four stage-coaches?"

Fargo remained silent but he smiled inwardly. Dockerby was shrewd enough to be cautious. "Business," Melanie said. "I've inherited some money and I want to start a stage line. My father worked for John Butterfield." She paused and waved a hand to Fargo. "This is Skye Fargo. He's going to be my partner. He'll be running our new line."

Dockerby's eyes flicked to Fargo and took him in with a sharp glance of his little eyes. "My plea-sure," he said and Fargo smiled back.

"We've studied the land and some maps. We think there's a need for a stage line that will run south along the edge of the Salmon River Moun-tains and down into Utah," Melanie said. "That way we won't be competing with any of the big lines. We want to start with four stages, all full Concords. Is that too much for you?"

"No, no," Dockerby said, his little eyes lighting up.

"Of course, we'd want to have a look at them," Fargo said.

"I've two you can have right now. I'll show you," the man said and Fargo strode beside Melanie as she followed Dockerby to the largest of the sheds. He motioned to two of the men at the bunkhouse and they hurried forward to open the shed doors and light two big lamps hanging on a wall. Fargo's eyes moved slowly across the four Concords in a row, all newly painted, he noted. "You can have these two right now," Dockerby said of the last two coaches in the row.

"What about the other two?" Melanie asked.

"They're sold. They're waiting to be picked up," Dockerby said.

"I want to take all four at once," Melanie said flatly.

Dockerby paused, but only for a moment. "All right, I can have two more for you in a week," he said.

"A week won't cause a problem," Melanie said with a glance at Fargo. He smiled and nodded back.

"These new?" he asked Dockerby, gesturing to the stages.

"New and reconditioned," Dockerby lied. "But they're all in top shape, guaranteed, all real Abbot and Downing Concords."

"That's good," Fargo said blandly.

"I can give you a down payment," Melanie told Dockerby.

"Wonderful. Come to the house," Dockerby said, his coarse face looking as pleased as it could. Fargo hurried after him with Melanie. They found themselves in a sparsely furnished house, where Melanie counted out a thousand dollars in bills that Fargo had given her, Buzz Collins's money, and Fargo smiled at the irony of it. Dockerby gave her a receipt as he quickly pocketed the cash.

"We'll be staying at the hotel," Melanie told Dockerby as they walked outside. "Call me as soon as the other two stages arrive."

"Yes, of course," Dockerby said.

"I may explore some trails while we're waiting," Fargo said.

"Good idea," Dockerby said and Fargo's eyes went to the men waiting by the bunkhouse.

"You've a big crew," he remarked.

"Ranch hands. Always can use extra ranch hands," Dockerby answered and waved as he rode away with Melanie. Fargo waited till they were past the bunkhouse before giving voice to his thoughts.

"Ranch hands, only there's no ranch," he said wryly.

"They're his stage raiders?" Melanie said.

"That's right. Maybe they steal the other wagons he sells, too. Wouldn't surprise me any." Fargo grunted. He led the way to the hotel. "I'll stable the horses. You get the rooms. Separate rooms. Everything proper," he said.

"Of course," Melanie said as she slid from her horse. Fargo left and found the public stable and paid the stableman for a week's stay. Melanie was waiting when he returned. She dropped his room key into his hand. "Separate," she said, her smile slightly smug, "but adjoining." He refused to echo her smile and they ate in a very quiet, decorous dining room at the hotel. Afterward they went to their rooms and when Melanie knocked at the door between the rooms she was surprised to see him still dressed.

"I'm going to check the maker's numbers on those coaches," Fargo said. "I want to be sure."

"Yes, of course," Melanie said, alarm rushing into her face. "Good God, what if they're not Buzz Collins's stages? What'll that mean?"

Fargo's lips tightened in a grimace. "I'm not wrestling with that till I have to," he said and started for the door. "I don't expect I'll be long."

"I hope not," she said much too softly as he hurried from the room. He walked through the dark, silent town, the only sound a distant tinkle of noise from the saloon. Dockerby's place was still and dark, the bunkhouse lights out. Still, he edged his way in a crouch, reached the long shed, and inched the door open. Inside, he paused to let his eyes adjust to the blackness, not daring to light one of the big wall lamps. Groping his way, he reached the row of Concords, knelt down beside the first one, and crawled under it. A coachmaker usually marked individual coach numbers on the underside of the coach, between the wide leather strips they called thorough braces that cradled the body of the coach. The usual spot was at the rear curve of the coach just below where the body and the rear boot joined together.

Only when he was well under the big Concord, lying on his back, did he light one of the long lucifers he had brought with him. He held the light up, peered at the underside of the coach, and ran his fingers along the place where the identifying numbers would be. Then he scooted himself sideways under the next coach, then the next, until he was under the last. The match burned out just as he finished examining the coaches and he carefully returned the burned-out portion to his pocket. Crawling from under the Concord, he left the shed, quietly closing the door as he did.

Melanie sat up as he entered the hotel room, her question instant. "The numbers matched, right?" she asked.

"No," he said. "But they're Collins's stages." Melanie stared at him. "The numbers have all been filed away. Don't you see, that's its own proof. The numbers wouldn't be erased if the coaches hadn't been stolen."

"No, I guess not," Melanie agreed. "So are we going to start back to tell Collins tomorrow?"

"That'd be condemning another stage of innocent passengers to death," Fargo said. "You gave Dockerby orders for two coaches. He's going to start filling it tomorrow."

"Oh God," Melanie whispered, dismay sweeping through her face.

"I'm not going to let that happen. I'm going after Dockerby's men. I'll be there when they attack their next stage," Fargo said.

Her eyes brightened. "That will be our chance to find out what they did with the last passengers,

Lucy and the others," Melanie said. "Maybe our only chance. I'll go with you."

"No, you've got to stay here and play out your role, let Dockerby see you, maybe visit him a few times. We don't want him getting suspicious. He's pretty damn shrewd," Fargo said.

She fell silent, acceptance in the unhappiness of her face. "Find out about Lucy. Make that your most important thing," she said.

"I'll tell you whatever I find out soon as I get back," he said.

"Promise?"

"Promise," he echoed. He undressed and lay down with her. She came to him with an intensity that transformed the night into a place of ecstasy revisited, passion renewed. Finally she slept cradled against him, waking only when he rose with the morning. He washed and dressed, not hurrying, and saw the question in her eyes. "I want to give them some distance. I don't want to crowd them," he told her and finished dressing.

"Good luck," she said, warm against him in her lovely nakedness, the intensity of the night still there in the way she clung to him. He left, reluctantly, he admitted to himself, and hurried to the stable and retrieved the Ovaro. He detoured, halting on a small rise that let him see Dockerby's place. Only four men lounged outside the bunkhouse and he grunted, satisfied. Things were moving as he expected. Dockerby had sent his men on their way. Fargo rode through town, searching the ground only when he reached the roads near the river landings. He rode slowly and it took him a while to sort through the prints and tracks that led from town. Finally, he spied what he sought, the clustered tracks of at least a half-dozen horses staying together. The tracks led down a road lined with box elder and white fir.

The further they got away from town, the easier they were to follow, and Fargo stayed back, content to read their tracks. When night came, he moved closer, close enough to see the figures start to make camp in a small clearing. Eight, he counted, swearing softly to himself and backing away to find his own spot to bed down. As he lay waiting for sleep, he frowned in thought. He couldn't see them going all the way back into Montana to hijack another stage. Distance and time would work against that. But perhaps they had no other choice. Whatever they did, he'd dog their steps, he grunted as sleep came to him. Morning brought him a moment of grim satisfaction as once again he tracked their path and saw their tracks suddenly turn north toward Ajax Mountain.

It was late afternoon when the long, winding road appeared, curving past high mountain terrain, and Fargo slowed. He saw the ground rutted with wheel marks. He dismounted, studied each of the tracks that were defined enough, and saw they were all the same width, all made by the same wagon or wagons of the same type. That made sense. Concords using the road would leave very similar marks. The road was plainly traveled by a stage line from the north. Dockerby obviously liked to travel further to steal his stages but Melanie had spurred him onto risking a closer strike. Returned to the saddle, Fargo moved the pinto slowly up past the road and into narrow mountain passages until he spotted the figures below, scattered among the trees and rocks bordering the road. Three were on their horses, the rest on foot, some were standing, others were on one knee, all were plainly waiting.

Fargo eased the Ovaro through a crevice in the rocks until he found a spot that gave him a clear view of all the figures below. Perhaps an hour had passed before Fargo caught the sound, hoofbeats reverberating through the mountainous terrain long before the stage came into sight. The waiting ambushers snapped to attention and Fargo pulled the big Henry from its rifle case. The men below were waiting to kill, as they had killed before, without hesitation and without pity. He had no choice but to stop them with the same ruthlessness and he let his eyes move from one waiting killer to the next until he had each one's position firmly imprinted in his mind.

He knew how they'd strike. They'd stop the stage, make it seem an ordinary holdup. Once the stage was stopped, they'd order the passengers out, then take down the driver and replace him. They wanted no more runaway stages. Fargo had the rifle raised as the stagecoach appeared. It was a full Concord with baggage on the roof rack. A lone driver, a gray-bearded man, held the reins of a six-horse team. He wasn't hurrying his horses and pulled them to a halt immediately as the two figures stepped out on the road in front of him, rifles raised and aimed. One of the ambushers took hold of the cheekstrap on the left lead horse.

"Everybody out," the other ordered while a

third man in a tan Stetson stepped out from behind a tree, a six-gun in his hand. The door of the stage opened and two men came out, both wearing suits and holding briefcases. Traveling salesmen, Fargo guessed. A woman came out next, clutching two boys Fargo guessed to be between four and six years old. An elderly man with a cane was the last to come from the stage. Fargo's glance darted across Dockerby's men and again took in those behind trees and rocks. He saw one raise his rifle and take aim at the stage driver. The moment had come, Fargo thought to himself bitterly and pressed the trigger on the big Henry. The man flew backward from his horse. The others, reacting with instant surprise, turned to glance at the man as he hit the ground. Two of them tried to turn back but the Henry barked again. They went down in unison, as though pulled by an invisible puppeteer.

This time the others dived for cover. Another two didn't make it as Fargo fired again from his vantage point. Five, he counted off in grim silence. But the two men who had stopped the coach bolted forward, knocked the woman down, and snatched up the two boys. Each holding one of the boys, they backed away from the road into thick tree cover. The last remaining dry-gulcher alive, in the tea Stetson, took refuge behind a white fir and called out. "One more shot and the kids get it," he threatened.

"No," the woman screamed. She started to run forward and fell, clutching her leg as a shot rang out. Fargo cursed silently. His advantage had been snatched away, the last three figures in tree cover he couldn't penetrate. He waited, motionless and silent, his eyes fixed on the trees where the trio were positioned. The tan hat's voice came again.

"You up there, whoever the hell you are, throw your gun down and come out or the kids get it," he said.

But Fargo had already slid from the saddle and put the Henry into its case. The Colt in hand, he moved through the trees that led down a narrow passage. "Now, dammit, throw your gun out," the man demanded. But Fargo let silence answer as he moved down the path, halting at a spot across from where the three men were dug in. He cursed again at this unexpected turn of events. One of the children whimpered and he shot a glance at the passengers. They were huddled alongside the stage with the woman, who lay on the ground, red seeping through her dress from her leg. The stage driver sat unmoving, clutching the reins in his hand. The tan Stetson's voice rose again. "We'll kill them, you bastard," he said again. "You think we're kidding, you'll find out different."

They weren't kidding, Fargo knew. They were cold-blooded killers but they understood the value of hostages. Hostages were shields, the last chips they had to play. They wouldn't throw away their last chips. It was a dangerous game he had to play, Fargo realized, yet he had no choice. Giving in to them would mean death for everyone. He had to play the deadly game to its end and hope he could put the right finish to it. He stayed behind the tree trunk as he raised his voice. "Let the boys go and you ride away alive. Hurt them and you're dead. Count on it," he said.

Silence followed, then he picked up the rustling of leaves, the muffled sounds of tense whispers following. He prayed that the men were not beyond logic, that the desperate still put survival over everything else. He felt the tiny beads of perspiration form on his forehead as he waited. His answer came with suddenness and another surprise. Footsteps came first, then bodies crashing through the trees, and then the sound of hoofbeats. They had elected to combine the best of their options, flight and the hostages.

Fargo took a moment to sort out sounds. Three horses, quickly separating from each other. He raced up the passage at his back and leaped onto the Ovaro. From the high hills he glimpsed the horse and rider racing north, the small figure draped facedown over the saddle. Cursing, Fargo sent the Ovaro down the passage, turning onto a path that paralleled the fleeing horseman. Keeping the Ovaro in a full gallop on the narrow and dangerously rutted road, he turned into a passage that took him down to the road below. Time was vital, he realized. He had to take risks he didn't want to take and as he closed in on the fleeing rider he brought the Colt up and let the Ovaro overtake the other horse. The man turned in the saddle, fired three shots and then a fourth. But Fargo lay low on the pinto's powerful jet black neck and the bullets hurtled past.

He let the Ovaro close in still further and saw the man turn to fire again, fear in his face now. Leaning forward, Fargo fired from between the pinto's ears, two shots and the rider in front of him jerked upward, his arms flailing the air. Fargo was almost at him as he toppled from the saddle. Bringing the Ovaro alongside the other horse, he leaned over in the saddle, grabbed the little boy by the back of his shirt, and pulled him onto the pinto. Reining to a halt, Fargo felt the small arms clinging tightly to him. "It's over, son. You're all right," he murmured. He stayed in place for a moment until he felt the youngster's grip relax. "Let's got back to your ma," he said and turned the horse in a tight circle.

He didn't bother to glance at the figure on the ground as he put the pinto into a trot, the boy holding tight to him as they rode. He retraced his steps and finally reached the huddled figures beside the stagecoach. They had bandaged the woman's leg, he saw, and she was able to stand leaning against the coach. He lowered the boy who raced, his little legs churning, into his mother's arms. "One more coming up," Fargo said as he sent the pinto downhill again. He returned to where the men had separated and fled and let his eyes sweep the ground until he found the second set of tracks. They went south, prints dug deep into the soil, the horse galloping hard. Fargo followed, keeping the Ovaro at a gallop without extending him fully, confident they'd still be gaining. The man had gone down onto flatland, allowing him to make better time across terrain dotted by sagebrush.

Fargo followed, read the trail without slowing, and as he rode, his thoughts went to the third man in the tan Stetson. Fargo wanted him alive and able to answer Melanie's questions about the passengers. But he'd have to hunt him down later.

The boy came first. Perhaps a half hour later the hoofprints leaped up at him. The man had taken a sharp turn left. With the canniness of a fugitive, he had sent the horse into a long stand of yellow-hued aspen. He knew the forest soil was covered with a deep growth of weeds, moss, and leaves that would mask clear prints. Fargo uttered a grim half laugh. The man didn't know the other signs that were as much part of a trailsman's wisdom as hoofprints, the branches on low brush still pushed back, the ends of low branches snapped off by an onrushing horse, the small whorls of loose leaves made by the wind of a galloping horseman.

They were there, all of them, as Fargo went through the forest, finally emerging on open land. He pressed the Ovaro, felt the horse respond with its powerful stride, and suddenly he caught sight of his quarry. He too had the boy draped face-down over the saddle, Fargo saw. He saw a long stretch of deep downy bromegrass and he veered onto it, letting it muffle the sound of the Ovaro's galloping hooves. The man didn't become aware of him until he was almost abreast of him and then fear and surprise drained the color from his face. But with a snarl he yanked his horse to the left and reined up at the edge of a stand of red ash. Fargo saw him jam his gun against the back of the boy's head.

"Stay back or he's dead, damn you, he's dead," the man shouted.

Fargo pulled his horse to a halt and cursed silently. It was a turn he hadn't expected. The man had come apart. He was past reaching, past reason. He hadn't gotten away and now he knew only desperation fed by fear and fury. Panic gripped him, unpredictable and dangerous. There was no telling what he might do. Fargo sat very still on his horse. "Easy now," he said quietly.

"Drop your gun," the man said, his pistol still held to the boy's head. "The gun, damn you." Fargo heard the click of the hammer being pulled back.

"Here," he said and threw the Colt out onto the grass. The boy didn't move, he noted gratefully.

"Get off the horse," the man ordered. He still held the gun against the boy and Fargo risked a long moment. On the ground he'd be completely at the man's mercy. Only there'd be no mercy. That was for certain. Yet he didn't dare refuse the order, didn't dare try to make a break for it on the Ovaro. The man would shoot. He was on the edge. Anything could set him off. All he had to do was to tighten his finger on the trigger, even inadvertently, and the boy was dead.

Fargo's jaw muscles twitched as he made his decision, if he could call it that. He'd have but one chance for the boy and for himself. The first objective was to get the gun from the boy's head. "I said get off, dammit," the man shouted. "I'll kill the damn kid." Fargo swung one leg slowly over the saddle, keeping the Ovaro between himself and the man. But as he dismounted behind the horse, his hand slid up his trouser leg and retrieved the thin throwing knife from its calf holster. Tucking the blade into the palm of his hand, he finished dismounting. The throw had to be underhand, he knew. He'd neither the time nor the room for anything else. "Get away from the horse," the man ordered.

"Yes, sir," Fargo said and peering over the saddle, saw the one thing he wanted to see above all else as the man took the gun from the boy's head and started to bring it around to point at his target. It had to all work perfectly, Fargo knew. There'd not be another chance. The man had his gun up but not aimed yet, Fargo saw. With his left hand, he slapped the Ovaro on the rump. The horse sprang forward as Fargo's right hand was already sending the double-edged blade through the air. The knife just cleared the horse's tail as Fargo dropped to the ground. The man started to aim his six-gun, his eyes searching for his target when he saw the blade hurtling at him. He started to twist away but he was too late. The razor-sharp blade, thrown with every last bit of strength Fargo possessed, slammed into his side. It buried itself in his rib cage, so deep it stopped only when the hilt brought it to a shuddering halt.

His finger tightened on the trigger as he pitched forward, sending two bullets harmlessly into the ground before he fell facedown. He let go of the gun and tried to grab awkwardly back at the blade sticking from his side. But his hand slid from the handle and he drew his last, gasping breaths. Fargo pushed himself to his feet and started forward as the boy slid from the saddle. The shot rang out and Fargo felt it go past his ear. He flung himself backward, twisting, and hit the ground as another shot grazed his shoulder. He rolled into the trees and rolled again. When he came up alongside the trunk of a red ash, he peered out through the foliage. The figure came out of the opposite row of trees, the tan Stetson pushed back on his head.

"Come out, mister," the man said, swinging down from his horse. "You can't get away."

Fargo swore at himself. He had underestimated the man. "Very smart. You figured I'd go after the boy," he said.

"It was a sure thing. I followed Jack the minute he took off with the kid. I just hung back. Jack didn't know I was behind him. You showed up sooner than I thought you would. You didn't spot me. You were too busy watching Jack," the man said. Fargo snorted bitterly and swore at himself again. "Come out. Don't make me go get you and maybe I'll let you walk," the man said.

"Sure, and you'll bake me a cake," Fargo said.

"Look, my boss is going to ask questions, who and why. Talk and you walk. We can deal," the man said.

Fargo smiled at the man's attempt to sound reasonable. He'd deal with a bullet. Fargo grunted and his eyes found the boy on the ground, looking on in terror. Returning his eyes to the tan Stetson, Fargo stepped from behind the tree. "Come get me," he called and began to move away. He made no effort to be quiet as he moved through the trees and saw the figure start to rush into the trees after him. He moved in a zigzag pattern for another minute and then came to a halt on one knee. He watched and saw the figure in the trees was moving, but with slow steps, halting to listen after every few paces. He was smart, Fargo saw, no bulling his way forward noisily. Fargo rose, moved, and brushed against a low branch. The man spun at once and started after him.

But the tan Stetson didn't move in a straight line. He came forward in a sideways pattern that let him cover a wide area as he continued to pause and listen with each step. Fargo swore silently. If he continued to stay motionless, the man would come upon him sooner or later. If he moved on, his pursuer would zero in on him fast enough. Fargo took another dozen careful, silent steps. But he knew he'd not be able to keep absolutely silent. There was always a hidden twig to crack, a loose stone to roll. Only the cougar and the lynx could walk the forest in total stillness. Crouching, he glimpsed his pursuer moving closer and he raised his eyes to an old, thick-branched box elder. A grim smile touched his lips. He reached up, closed his hands around the ridged, gray-brown bark, and lifted himself upward until he could wrap a leg around the adjoining branch.

He brought his other leg up and sat on the branch as he picked out the figure below still moving carefully in his sweeping pattern. Fargo shifted position and brought both legs up onto the branch until he was perched atop it. Below, the tan Stetson came forward again, searching, listening, the six-gun ready. Fargo waited and let him come another dozen steps. The man paused again, listening as his eyes probed the trees and low brush. Fargo grimaced. The man wasn't precisely under the branch but he was probably as close as he was going to be.

Fargo jumped from his perch in an almost vertical leap. The branch dipped, then sprang back into place with an infuriating noisiness. The man spun at once and started to bring his gun up, but Fargo was already smashing into him, both feet crashing into his shoulders. The figure went sprawling, his shot going wild into the air, and Fargo hit the ground on his hands and knees, the pain shooting through him. Pushing to his feet, he saw the man starting to get up, still shaking the cobwebs from his head. Fargo's long, looping right crashed into his jaw and he went down again, the gun falling from his hand. Fargo scooped up the pistol and turned it on the figure slowly regaining his feet, one hand holding his jaw. The man lifted his eyes, resignation in them. "Go on, get it over with," he said.

"You're a lucky man. You've another chance to stay alive," Fargo said. "If you give me straight answers. Start walking, ahead of me. Fargo saw the relief in the man's eyes as he began to go through the trees. "You have a name?" Fargo asked.

"Matson, Tom Matson," the man said. Fargo emerged from the trees behind him. The boy was still frozen in place.

"Come over here, son," he called and the boy came running. Fargo lifted him onto the Ovaro with a reassuring smile. "You'll be back with your ma soon," he said, bending down and scooping up the Colt. Emptying Matson's gun, he threw the weapon into the trees.

"Who the hell are you, mister?" Matson asked.

"Robin Hood. The tooth fairy. It's not important," Fargo said and used his lariat to bind Matson's wrists in front of him. Then he motioned for him to get on his horse. "We'll be riding and you'll be talking," Fargo said. "But first we take the boy back to his ma."

Keeping Matson in front of him, Fargo rode with the boy and set an unhurried pace as he retraced his steps to where the stage still waited, its driver and passengers beside it. The boy leaped from the Ovaro and raced into his mother's arms. After holding him tight, the woman's eyes lifted and she went to Fargo. "I'll never be able to thank you enough," she said.

"You just have." He smiled. "Now you can go on getting these folks to where they were going," he said to the driver.

"What in tarnation was this all about and how'd you come to be here, mister?" the driver asked.

"You got yourselves caught in the middle of something else. It's over, knowing more won't help you any," Fargo said. He motioned to Matson as he spurred the Ovaro forward and the man rode in front of him. "Trot," Fargo ordered as he set a faster pace. Turning east, he headed the long way back to the Montana Territory. He didn't question the man any further until night came and he found a spot to camp. After letting Matson eat, he tied him again, this time his ankles as well as his wrists. "How long has Dockerby been stealing stagecoaches?" Fargo questioned as he stretched out on the ground.

"I've worked for him for a year," the man answered. "Where do you fit in this, mister?"

"I'll ask the questions," Fargo said. "How many innocent passengers have you killed?" The man's face tightened and he didn't answer. "Where are the passengers from the last stage you brought Dockerby from Montana?" Fargo questioned.

"Buried," the man said.

"Their things?"

"With them."

"Where?" Fargo growled, his voice suddenly ice.

"About a thousand yards back of where you came onto the runaway stage. There's a thick stand of dwarf maple," Matson said.

"You can show me," Fargo said. He turned on his side and drew sleep around himself, the Colt tucked against his chest. He was confident that if Matson tried anything he'd hear it. The night deepened, weariness covering both men.

6

Morning dawned and Fargo continued the trek east, staying close behind his prisoner. It was nearing an end. He should be feeling satisfied, congratulating himself on a job well done, he told himself. But he didn't feel that way. He felt uneasy and unsatisfied, as though there was more than what he had found. The little things that had stabbed at him at the start were still there, still stabbing. Little things had a way of doing that, throbbing, irritating, unwilling to go away, refusing to be pushed aside. As he rode on, the inner frown stayed with him and he continued to wonder why he wasn't more satisfied.

Matson rose wrapped in the silence of a man who had accepted his fate and Fargo was grateful for that. It was midafternoon when Fargo reached the place where he had first seen the runaway stage. Matson guided him down to the thick stand of dwarf maple. "In there," said with a nod of his head.

Fargo's lips tightened as he felt the combination of anger and disgust sweep through him. "Bastard," he bit out. "All of you."

"It was just a job." The man shrugged and Fargo fought to keep his rage in check. The man didn't even have the decency to feel a shred of remorse. Fargo didn't take to six-gun justice but he was tempted and made himself turn away.

"Let's go. There's a rope waiting for you," he said and rode close behind Matson as they went east again. They reached Bolton Flats with perhaps an hour of daylight left and he took Matson to the sheriff first. He gave the lawman enough to have him put the man behind bars. Fargo's next stop was Buzz Collins and Leah opened the door. She threw her arms around him instantly. He'd almost forgotten how striking she was with her pale skin and onyx hair. She stepped back and led him into the house and called out to her brother. Buzz Collins hurried into the living room and his darting eyes searched Fargo's face. "I found your stages," Fargo said and Collins let out a roar of delight.

"All four of them?" he asked and Fargo nodded.

"Jesus, that's news, real news," Buzz Collins said. "Where are they?"

"Place called Elkton, in Idaho Territory," Fargo said and told him of Harry Dockerby's business built on stolen stages.

"That son of a bitch. He's as good as dead," Collins roared. "How many men has he got?"

"A lot less than he had since my last meeting with his boys. I'd say he still has some six men," Fargo estimated.

Collins thought for a moment. "I'll get a dozen. That'll give me four drivers on the way back. I want to bring all four of my coaches back at once. I'll get me a dozen good shots," he said.

"No, not till I go back there first," Fargo said.

"Why?" Collins frowned.

"I've got to get somebody out of there. She's been a real help. You go charging in, Dockerby will put two and two together and kill her. I want to get her out first," Fargo said.

"You get her out and this Dockerby will get suspicious. He'll take off or worse, burn the stages. No stages, no evidence. He could deny everything. She stays. I get my stages first," Collins said.

"Sorry, I'm getting her out of there first. She's risking her neck being there now," Fargo insisted.

"No, goddammit," Collins said, his thin nose quivering. "Screw the girl. She'll have to take her chances. I want those stages."

Fargo felt his anger explode. This was more of the man's selfish, callous attitude. "Screw you. Melanie first. You hold off till I get to her," Fargo said. He brushed past Collins and Leah as he started for the door. "I want a full day's start," he threw back. He didn't see the blow coming. It landed hard on the back of his head and yellow lights flashed through him. Dimly, he was aware of falling and then the blackness closed over him.

When consciousness returned, it sent out little harbingers, eyelids fluttering, a sharp pain spearing through his head. Fargo pulled his eyes open and stared up at flat grayness. The grayness became a ceiling and he pushed up onto his elbows, glanced around, and saw that he was in a cellar that had been furnished as a room, a bed at one side and two chairs and a table. Windowless, the cellar had a lone door with a small, high window cut into it. He became aware of a strange, cloying odor in his nostrils and a dry, sourish taste in his mouth. He sat up, then pushed to his feet, the odor filling his nostrils. He took out his kerchief and blew his nose but it failed to go away. His eyes moved across the cellar, which was barren except for the few sticks of furniture, and felt his anger surging.

The argument swam back into his mind. Buzz Collins had struck him from behind, probably with a gun butt. The man's actions had been an echo of his callous disregard for the passengers he had revealed before. Buzz Collins wasn't simply anxious to get his stages back. He wasn't just desperate. He was obsessed, consumed with a towering selfishness. Fargo stepped to the door, closed a big hand around the doorknob, and turned. The door was locked from outside, probably a bolt, Fargo decided as he felt the knob turn. He raised himself to his full height and peered through the small, high window. There was a small alcove and a stairway behind it. Two men were seated on stools, obviously guards. Fargo pounded his fist on the door and both men looked up. "Where's Collins?" he questioned.

"Gone," the one man said.

"How long have I been here?" Fargo asked.

"Couple of hours," the guard answered. "The boss gave you a dose of chloroform before bringing you down here. He wanted you quiet for a while."

"Son of a bitch," Fargo bit out as he understood the odor and taste in his mouth and nostrils. The man's answer hung before him, its meaning all too clear. Collins and his posse were on their way.

Of course he'd need probably two days to reach Elkton, even with hard riding. But he couldn't get there first, Fargo told himself. There had to be a way out of the cellar. But he saw none as he turned and surveyed the room. His holster was empty, of course, he felt as his hand automatically went to it. But the knife was still in its calf holster around his leg. His eyes took in the bed against the wall. It was just beyond sight of anyone peering through the window.

Maybe there was a way out of the cellar, Fargo thought to himself as he returned to the door. "Tell Leah I want to talk," he said and peered through the window.

"I'm no messenger," one of the men said.

"You won't be anything if you don't tell her. She's waiting to hear from me," Fargo said. The man looked up and frowned, suddenly uncertain of his surliness. He rose and Fargo stepped away from the door as the guard trudged up the stairs. Lowering himself to the edge of the bed, Fargo waited. He banked on a combination of curiosity and memory to bring Leah down.

He smiled as he heard the footsteps from outside. He stood up as the door opened. Leah came in, the two guards with her. "Can we talk alone?" he said, putting just the right note of deference into his voice. Leah liked being in command. That had been clear in bed. Her little smile told him he was right.

"Wait outside," she said to the two guards but left the door slightly ajar as she turned back to him. "I'm sorry about what happened, Fargo. I'd no idea Buzz was going to get so angry. It all happened so quickly."

"Not your fault," Fargo said soothingly. "But you can get me out of here. I've got to get there first. He's risking a girl's life."

Sympathy flooded Leah's face. "I know how you feel but I can't go against Buzz. He's my brother. It's his show, his decisions. I can't go against that."

"I hoped you'd understand," Fargo said, letting reluctant acceptance mix with his disappointment.

"I do but I can't go behind Buzz's back. We do what we have to do," she said with a shrug and another sympathetic glance.

"Guess so," he said. He took a step closer, his hand closing around her shoulder, his thumb moving down to the swell of her breast. "I'm not happy but I guess I could settle for that promise you made," he said and saw the stirring darken her eyes as his hand slid down along the long curve of her breast. "You didn't forget, did you?" he asked.

"Of course not," she said. "Here?" she asked.

"Why not? I can't get out and we've plenty of time," he said. "I've been thinking plenty about it, figured you were too."

"Yes," she said, her voice turning husky as his hand moved quickly, cupping her breast. He heard the sharp intake of breath from her. He rubbed his thumb across her nipple, felt it already standing.

"Close the door," he murmured. She turned and stepped to the door and called to the guards.

"Lock the door and go upstairs. Come back in

an hour," she said and pushed the door shut. He heard the outside bolt slide into place and lowered himself on the bed.

"Only an hour?" he smiled as Leah came to him.

"I can send them away again," she said. He took his gunbelt off and started to undress.

"What happened to my Colt and my horse?" he asked casually.

"The gun's upstairs. Your horse is in the barn," Leah said. She began to unbutton her blouse and Fargo reached over and helped her shed the garment, then the skirt and slip. He stopped himself from hurrying, felt the frown touch his brow, and realized he had been hurrying for the wrong reasons. Her pale white skin shimmering, she came to him and he realized he was about to do something he'd never done before. He was going to make love to a beautiful woman and he didn't want to do it. He was going to immerse himself in her warm wanting when he wanted to be someplace else. The reasons were clear enough, all bringing him to the same point. All he could think about was reaching Melanie in time. But that wasn't enough. Leah's refusal to undo her brother's actions angered him. It somehow made her a party to his callousness and he had to wonder about her part in everything.

As he shed his clothes and Leah pressed herself to him, he wondered if he could carry it off. But Leah and nature answered that. Tiny red nipples and glowing pink areoles answered that. An onyx triangle against pale white skin answered that. The long curve of breasts, the searing hotness of lips and tongue, the wet, warm touch of full thighs, and the dark softness of welcoming wanting answered that. He made love to Leah and found that though his heart wasn't in it every other part of him was and finally her screams of pleasure echoed through the cellar and he lay with her as she drew in deep breaths of pleasure fulfilled.

When he began to pull on his clothes, her eyes followed, faint questioning in their dark orbs. "I can send them away again," she said.

"No. I'll be leaving," he said. He saw the tiny furrow cross her brow as he finished dressing. The furrow became a frown and she sat up and peered hard at him. He said nothing but he knew the thoughts were coming together in her mind.

"You bastard," she hissed, reaching for her blouse.

He shrugged. "We do what we have to do," he said. "Sound familiar?" She swung at him and he caught her arm and spun her onto the bed.

"You did it all so I'd send the guards away," Leah said, pulling on her clothes. "But the door's locked and they're due back. You won't get anywhere, damn you."

"We'll see about that," Fargo said as she finished dressing. Her lunge took him by surprise, a quick, sweeping motion toward the door. He caught her, his short, chopping blow sharp on the point of her jaw knocked her out instantly. He carried her to the bed just as he heard the guards returning.

"We're back, Miss Collins," one called.

Drawing the knife from its calf holster, Fargo

pressed himself against the wall beside the door. "Miss Collins, you all right?" the other one called. Only silence answered. They were peering through the window now, he knew, but they couldn't see the bed or the wall where he was. "Miss Collins, talk to us," the guard called. Again, there was only silence.

"Something's wrong," the other one said. "We better go in." Fargo heard the bolt being pulled back, then the door flew open. The first guard half fell into the room, six-gun in hand. He never got a chance to turn as the point of the knife pushed into the back of his neck.

"Drop the gun," Fargo muttered. The man stiffened but he dropped the gun. The second guard was in the room. He turned, his gun raised to fire. Fargo stayed behind the other man, the knife held to his neck. "You fire and he's dead. He gets your bullet or my knife. Drop the gun or take your pick," Fargo said. The man hesitated, uncertain about what he should do.

"Drop the gun, for God's sake," the first guard hissed. The man let his gun fall from his hand.

"Back up, against the bed," Fargo ordered and the man obeyed. Fargo drew the point of the knife from the guard's neck, pushed and sent the man stumbling forward. He scooped up both guns as he backed up to the door. "She'll come around soon. You can all hold hands," he said, slamming the door shut and sliding the bolt on. He took the stairs two at a time, ran into the main part of the house, and found his Colt in a side room. He emptied the guards' guns, left them, and ran from the house. The Ovaro was in the stable on a loose tether, the saddle on the floor and in minutes, Fargo was on the horse and racing into the night. He turned the pinto west, settled the horse into a smooth, steady pace. Collins and his posse had a good start on him but he had his advantages. He knew the way. They'd be exploring. And a lone rider could make better time than a group. He rode through the dark until he reined up at a spot between two high rocks and camped for the night. He fell asleep at once and awoke with his energy restored.

He found a patch of wild plums for breakfast and returned to a steady pace. He didn't bother to search for signs of Collins and his men. He rode through passages he knew, staying away from the river until the day was nearing an end. When he turned downhill, he halted when he glimpsed the river to his left, bedded down under a peach leaf willow, and quickly fell asleep. He had passed Collins somewhere, he was certain, but he didn't know by how much. The men could be close behind. There'd be no time to relax. But he'd reach Melanie first and he allowed himself a sigh of relief for that.

When morning came he held to his pace and rode into Elkton with the noon sun and went straight to the hotel. He called out as he knocked on the door of Melanie's room. "Open up, it's me," he said. The door pulled open and he found himself staring into the barrels of two Remington-Beals single-action service revolvers.

"Don't bother unpacking," one of the men, a short, burly figure, said. "Mr. Dockerby's waiting for you." Fargo felt the pit of his stomach contract.

Something had gone wrong. The other man reached out and took his Colt as the first one prodded him in the chest with the Remington. "Start walking," the man ordered. "Nice and easy." Both men stayed just behind him as he walked from the hotel and Fargo saw one bring the Ovaro along as they trudged to Dockerby's place. The men took him to the long shed and pushed him inside, where Harry Dockerby frowned at him, his thick, heavy face darkened with suspicion. Fargo's eyes went past the man and he saw Melanie, her arms tied to a chair. In her eyes he saw a combination of fear, apology, and despair.

"Where's the stage I ordered?" Dockerby asked Fargo.

"It won't be coming," Fargo said.

"I was afraid of that. But I knew if it didn't come, you would," Dockerby said. "Soon as I found out about little Melanie I knew that."

Fargo's eyes went to Melanie. "My fault," she said, her voice breaking. "I messed up."

"I questioned her about her plans. She came up with all the wrong answers. Then one of my men found Horgan's raft. Little Melanie ran out of lies," Dockerby said. "And now you've run out of time, both of you."

"You're the one out of time," Fargo said. "Matson talked. There's a posse of gunslingers on their way, I'd guess they'll be riding in anytime now. Buzz Collins is bringing them. He wants his stages back and you dead." Dockerby's eyes narrowed as they searched Fargo's face. "I came back to get

Melanie before all hell breaks loose," Fargo said and Dockerby continued to peer at him.

"How many?" one of the men asked.

"More than enough. A dozen, maybe more," Fargo said.

"We didn't sign on to fight off a posse," the man said to Dockerby. "We're not hanging around for that."

"How do you know he's not lyin'?" Dockerby said, but his eyes stayed on Fargo.

Fargo gave a half snort. "Stick around and find out," he said.

"He's not lyin'," one of the men said. "We're cutting out." Both men turned and strode from the shed as they tossed Dockerby the Colt. Fargo saw Dockerby lick his thick lips, nervousness pushing hard at him.

"You've one chance. Run," Fargo said.

"Sure, and have you tailing me?" the man said.

"I won't be coming after you," Fargo said.

"I know you won't. Neither will Collins," Dockerby said, backing up to where Melanie sat. He pulled the knot holding her ropes open. "I'll be taking her with me while you wait for Collins and his gunslingers. When they get here, you're going to tell them which way I'm headed."

"Only it'll be all a false lead," Fargo said.

"You catch on fast. I'll tell you what to tell them. You make sure you do it, make sure they believe you. Collins finds me, she's dead," Dockerby said and Fargo swore silently. With the desperate cleverness of the cornered rat, Dockerby had thrown it all into his lap and Fargo could only curse at the irony of his helping the man escape. "Get over to that wagon wheel," Dockerby said and gestured with the Colt. Fargo stepped over to the wheel. "Tie him to the rim," Dockerby ordered Melanie. With helplessness in her eyes, she took the rope he had tied her with and began to bind Fargo's wrists to the wheel. Dockerby stood close and watched her carefully. "Tighter," he snapped at one point. Finally she was finished and Dockerby inspected the ropes.

"You tell Collins that I've gone up north along the Beaverhead Range. There's an old Shoshone trail. Then I'm turning west toward the Salmon River canyon. Tell him I've a cabin just below Lost Trail Pass," Dockerby said, pulling Melanie with him as he started for the door. "Remember, he finds me, she's dead," the man said and pushed Melanie out the door with him. The sound of their hoofbeats came moments after and quickly died away. Fargo tried to pull free of the ropes and found they were too well tied. He tried using his teeth to pull the knot open but it refused to yield. Almost two hours passed and he was still struggling to free himself when he heard the deep rumble of hooves in a pack. He listened to them come to a halt outside the shed.

His eyes were on the door as it flew open and Collins burst in, followed by a dozen men. Collins halted and his jaw dropped open as he saw Fargo. "How the hell did you get here?" he asked, recovering from his surprise.

"Cut me loose," Fargo said and Collins used a pocket knife to cut the ropes. "Leah let me go," Fargo said.

"No. She wouldn't. She didn't," Collins said firmly.

"Maybe not exactly," Fargo conceded. "Let's say she couldn't turn down a good lay."

"Damn her," Collins said, plainly able to accept that explanation. "Where's Dockerby?" he asked.

"Gone. But I know where. I heard him tell one of his men," Fargo said earnestly, mindful that he had to be convincing.

"Never mind," Collins said, turning to the four stages. "These my coaches?"

"Yes," Fargo said. "You're not going after Dockerby?"

"No. I don't give a shit where he's gone. Maybe I'll catch up with him someday, someplace. Right now I'm taking my stages back," Collins said and began to bark orders to his men, ordering the horses unsaddled and hitched to the coaches. Fargo backed quietly away as Collins gave all his attention to the stages. He slipped from the shed and saw the Ovaro where Dockerby's men had left it. But the rifle was gone from its case. Fargo pulled himself onto the horse. Dockerby's cleverness had become undone because of Collins's obsession with his stages. Irony on top of irony.

He sent the Ovaro forward. There was no time to hunt up a gun. There was time only to find Dockerby and he knew he was making a guess as he turned the horse south. Dockerby had gone to great lengths to send Collins north, then west and north again. Meanwhile, Dockerby could have gone anywhere. But he was clever, not smart. Fargo wagered that Dockerby would do the unimaginative and go exactly opposite to where he had tried to send Collins. With the instincts of a thief not a woodsman, he'd think that was the smart thing to do.

Fargo pulled on what he knew of the land and turned south when he left town. He planned to find a trail that followed the Lemhi River south, then turn west into the Beaverhead Range, then south again to the Jefferson River, everything the exact opposite of the route Dockerby had said he'd take. It was all wild and rugged land and there weren't that many trails. Dockerby wasn't the kind to make his own. He didn't have the skills or the stomach for that and when Fargo saw a narrow trail south through a forest of aspen, he took it. He set a steady pace, retracing his steps a few times when the trails he chose became barren, not a mark or sign to help on them. He was paralleling the Lemhi on a very winding trail covered with deer and elk prints when he spotted the hoofprints of two horses riding close together.

He smiled and spurred the Ovaro on as the day began to slide toward an end. Another narrowed trail crossed the one he was on; it turned west toward the Beaverhead. Fargo turned instantly toward it. He smiled again when he spotted the hoofprints. He halted, dismounted, and knelt down to examine the marks. They were fresher than he'd expected. He wasn't far behind them and when he returned to the saddle he grimaced at the dusk as it began to descend. In the light that was left, he scoured the land on both sides and didn't see any other trails. He elected to stay with the one he was on as night came to plunge the land into darkness.

He slowed the pinto to a walk, unwilling to risk a sudden turn and a sudden tree trunk. The moon finally rose high enough to penetrate the lush, dense woodland, but he kept the horse at a walk as he peered into the trees that crowded the trail. Dockerby hadn't the skill for night riding. He would have stopped by now, Fargo was certain and he dismounted and went further on foot as the Ovaro followed. The moon was fitful, the night a thing of shifting blackness. The forest became a black curtain that let the moonlight in almost with mocking delight as it wrapped its secrets in its leafy shroud. But once again he was the trailsman with the lore of the trail etched inside him. Like the silent mountain cats, he had more than one way to make his path through the night.

His nostrils quivered suddenly as smell, not sight, spoke silently to him. The odor of horses came to him, that special odor of horses still sweating from being ridden hard. He tied the Ovaro to a low branch and went on alone until an opening in the trees let the moonlight bathe a glen set back some hundred yards from the road. The average rider, trusting only his eyes, would have never seen it as he went by. Fargo shifted direction on careful, silent footsteps. When he reached the little glen, he saw the two figures asleep on the ground. He crept closer and saw Melanie lying uncomfortably, both her arms outstretched, a lariat tying her to a branch. Dockerby lay close by her and Fargo's eyes picked out the Colt at the man's side.

He drew the thin, razor-sharp throwing knife

from his calf holster, knowing he had only one weapon and one chance. He rose on one knee, measured the distance, and swore to himself. A sleeping figure was never a good target. The blade would have to go straight and then downward. Pausing to measure the distance again, he brought his arm back and sent the knife hurtling through the air. But the curse fell from his lips as the blade left his hand. Melanie took that instant to turn and pull at her ropes. Dockerby woke at once and sprang up to a sitting position. Fargo saw the knife graze the back of his shoulders and slam into the tree where Melanie was tied.

Dockerby turned back from Melanie as he felt the knife pass, surprise still freezing him for a moment. Fargo was hurling himself across the few yards, only seconds away from the man as he saw Dockerby bring the Colt up. Fargo hurled himself into a twisting ball as he dived sideways and the shot went past him, but only by a hair. He kicked out as he landed, his boot smashing into Dockerby's arm and the man's second shot went wild. Twisting his body again, he stuck an arm out stiffly. It hit Dockerby in the throat and the man went sideways, gagging hard. Still gagging, he tried to swing around, but Fargo's kick hit his wrist and the Colt went spinning from his grip. Fargo did a half somersault and came up on his feet in time to meet Dockerby's charge as the man bulled into him. The bull-like strength of the man was instant as Fargo went down backward, Dockerby's hand grasping for his throat. Bringing a short right up in a sideways arc, putting all the strength he could into the awkward motion, he sank the blow into Dockerby just below his ribs.

The man's breath rushed from him, his grip loosened, and Fargo flung him away and spun, throwing a roundhouse left from one knee. It landed against Dockerby's jaw and the man went sprawling backward. Fargo cursed again as he saw Dockerby land against the base of the tree and he leaped forward as the man reached up and pulled the knife from the tree trunk. Dockerby tried to bring the blade up from where he half sat, half lay on the ground. He missed as Fargo twisted his body to one side. Dockerby pushed himself forward to get to his feet, the knife clutched in his hand when Fargo's double-handed blow came down on the back of his neck.

The man pitched forward, a groaning sound rising from him. Slowly, his big body turned on its side. He was still clutching the knife but the blade was buried into his stomach. He lay, shuddered, and finally stopped.

Fargo rose to his feet and turned to Melanie. She had her face turned away. When he undid her ropes she fell against him and clung to him, but there was no trembling to her. "Let's get away from here," she said when she stepped back, still keeping her face from Dockerby's silent form.

"Get your horse," he said as he retrieved the knife and wiped it clean. Then he took his Colt and found the rifle on Dockerby's mount.

"How'd you find us?" Melanie asked when they began to slowly ride back.

"Figured out what he'd do, where he'd go. That was the easy part," Fargo told her.

"Collins show up to free you?" she asked.

Fargo nodded. "He's taking his stages back, probably leave come morning. He didn't say anything about her cousin or the other passengers. She'd had enough for now. He'd find a better time and place on the way back. As they rode, he realized something. She hadn't asked. Perhaps she knew, inside her. Perhaps there was no more looking away.

7

He slept late into the morning, Melanie beside him. They reached the Lemhi soon after they began to ride and used the river to wash. He skirted Elkton as he began the ride back to Montana Territory and set an unhurried pace. Yet before the day ended he had caught up to Collins moving his four Concords back home. "We'll be going around them," he told Melanie and took a high trail that curved south before it turned east again.

"Why?" she asked.

"Collins isn't happy with me. I'm not happy with him. I did my job. I'm through with the man," Fargo said.

"There's more," Melanie said flatly.

"It concerned you," he said.

"Tell me," she said.

He shrugged and told her how Collins had been totally unconcerned about her life. She thought for a moment before answering, her round-cheeked face more resigned than angry when she did. "That's his way. You said he'd shown no feeling for the passengers on his stage, only his damn coach. There are a lot of people like him, too many," she said.

Her answer brought all the questions that stayed inside him rushing forward, Collins's obsession with his Concords still refusing easy explanation. Of course, there were those who cared only about possessions and nothing about people. Collins plainly seemed to be one. Yet even that explanation failed to satisfy. Those who cared only about possessions were invariably greedy and tightfisted. They weren't the kind to pay more for the return of four stages than they were worth and that's what Collins had done. It still didn't fit. Melanie said nothing more and he rode in silence with her. They were nearing Bolton Flats when she finally voiced the question he'd waited to hear, coming at it obliquely when she did.

"You can stop holding back," she said and he shot a glance at her. Her face was tight and expressionless. "What did you find out about Lucy and the others. You can give it to me."

His lips pulled back in a grimace. Sometimes trying to soften things didn't help at all. "They're all dead," he said.

"Their things?" she asked.

"Buried with them," he said.

"Where?"

"Near where I found the runaway stage. Dockerby's man showed me," he said.

"Then you can take us there," she said and he nodded. "I'll get the others when we reach town," she added and said no more, but he noticed she put her horse into a trot and he followed. There was enough light left in the day when they reached Bolton Flats and he drew up outside the stage depot. "I'll be back," she said.

"Tell them to bring shovels," he said as she hurried away.

When she returned she had the others following and he looked a little like the Pied Piper on horseback. Rod Harris was first behind her, determination in his tight-lipped face. Winifred Bivins had left her child with someone and rode alone. Ralph Abel brought up the rear, a nervous eagerness in the way he sat his horse. All, including Melanie, carried shovels. They all swung in behind Fargo and he led the way from town, along the sagebrush-covered flatland and into the low hills where it all began. The road around the high rocks led him to the stand of dwarf maple and he brought the pinto to a halt in front of the trees and swung to the ground. They followed on his heels as he moved into the small trees, pushing forward, pointed and toothed leaves giving way. Well into the stand of maples, he saw where the ground grew suddenly disturbed, then, a dozen feet on, he found the two mounds, the soil hastily and sloppily piled up.

Melanie was the first to start digging, plunging her shovel into the first of the two mounds with an angry intensity. Rod Harris started digging along with her while Winifred Bivins and Ralph Abel attacked the second, larger mound. Fargo stood back, watching. Winifred Bivins and Ralph Abel had the harder of it, their mound not only much larger, but deeper and full of small rocks. When Melanie had only a small amount of dirt left to dig, Fargo stepped forward, put his hand over hers on the shovel. "Maybe I'd better finish," he said. She hesitated but relinquished the shovel and Fargo began digging. When he finished, Rod Harris across from him, he saw only one body lay in the pit, still in surprisingly good condition. Fargo stared down at a woman of some fifty years of age, he guessed, a stocky body with graying hair. She wore a black jacket over a black skirt. A thin, flat leather pouch lay atop her, obviously thrown in after her. Her fingers clutched a wallet-sized card.

"Damn," he heard Rod Harris hiss. Then he turned and began digging at the next mound with the others. Fargo reached down and pulled the card from the woman's fingers. It was an identification card with an emblem printed over the words. "Mildred Powell—Prison Board—Territory of Kansas," he read aloud. The frown slid across his brow as he looked at Melanie, then he reached down and took the flat, leather pouch from atop the woman's body.

"I'll take that," Melanie said sharply. But a wave of alarm and suspicion swept through Fargo and he pulled the pouch back, opened it, and drew out a sheet of paper. The alarm and astonishment spiraled through him as he stared at the piece of paper and took in the official stamp at the top of it.

"Melanie Carter," he read aloud, "this will verify that all official records of your past have been destroyed on orders of the Court, Judge Harold Waxman presiding, Territory of Kansas. In accordance with the terms agreed upon, this officially erases any charges and actions that have been on record against you. It further strikes from the record any evidence of your existence. You are now officially Sarah Wall. The papers herewith will provide you with all the background you will need as Sarah Wall. Board of Prisons—Territory of Kansas."

Still holding the letter, Fargo looked up at her, became aware that the others had stopped digging and were listening with rapt attention. "Cousin Lucy?" he said.

"I can explain," Melanie said.

"I'd like to hear that," he said.

"I went to work for a very powerful man in Missouri. But he wanted a lot more than work from me. He told me he could do whatever he wanted with me, that he and his family practically owned Missouri. He was right but I hated him. Finally, I wouldn't take it anymore. When he wouldn't stop, I shot him, five times. I told the judge I wasn't one damn bit sorry."

Fargo thought of her words after they'd first made love. "When there's something you have to do or want to do, you just do it. No questioning, no searching, no regretting. You just do it," he quoted.

She didn't smile but remembering was in her eyes. "That's right," she said. "Of course, they put me in jail. The family went all out to have me hanged. But I threatened to tell everything I knew about him and I'd learned a lot. They didn't want that. They agreed to my going free, saying it was all an accident. But I knew I'd never be safe. They had too much power. I didn't want them to ever be able to find me again. The Court agreed to do away with me as Melanie Carter, give me a new name, a new history, and a new existence."

"Cousin Lucy was all an invention, a damn lie," Fargo said.

"I had to get the papers buried with that prison officer. My new life was buried with her," Melanie said.

He handed her the pouch and everything in it. There didn't seem to be anything to say and he turned to the second, larger grave. Rod Harris and Ralph Abel began to dig again with renewed franticness. When Rod Harris moved aside the last shovelful of dirt at his side of the hole, he leaped down to the figure lying there. "Steven Tinsdale?" Fargo asked and Harris nodded as he pulled a leather briefcase out of the dead man's hand. Harris tried to jump out of the pit, missed his footing, and the case hit the edge of the grave, flew open, and Fargo stared down at the cascade of banknotes that spilled across the ground.

"Goddamn," Harris swore and frantically began to pull himself out of the pit. Some of the banknotes fluttered to Fargo's feet and he picked up a handful. They were all bearer notes that anyone could cash, none in sequence as they would have been in a bank payment.

"These your family documents?" Fargo asked.

"Give me those," Harris said with a snarl and lunged at Fargo. He wound up on his hands and knees as Fargo avoided the lunge and sank a short right into his stomach. He looked down at Harris as the man heaved to regain his breath. "They don't look like family documents to me, mister. They look like stolen bearer bonds to me, all carefully out of sequence," Fargo said.

"None of your goddamn business," Harris snarled as he pushed to his feet.

"Maybe no and maybe yes. Catching crooks is everybody's business," Fargo said. Harris started to scoop up the bonds, half turned away, and then spun around. Fargo saw the gun he yanked from under his vest, a Sharps four-barreled derringer, model four, a viciously effective little pistol. Fargo dropped flat before Harris had the Colt raised and he felt the bullet fly past his head. But his own Colt had left its holster with the speed of a rattler's strike as Fargo fired from his prone position. The derringer flew into the air as Harris grabbed at his hand in pain. "It just became my business," Fargo said, pushing to his feet.

Harris glowered at him as he pressed his hand against his chest, pain and fury wreathing his face. "I need a doc," he said.

"First the sheriff," Fargo said and turned to where Ralph Abel lowered himself into the gravesite where a man's body lay against the wall of the pit, an envelope in his hand. Abel pulled the envelope free, turned and immediately pulled himself out of the hole. "Aren't you going to spend a half minute with your brother?" Fargo asked. Ralph Abel paused and frowned. "That doesn't show much brotherly love," Fargo said and Ralph Abel glowered at him. "Could it be because he's not your brother?" Fargo pressed. Cold anger swept through the man's face. "Did you lie to me about that?" Fargo questioned. He took a step forward as the man didn't answer. Fargo's hand shot out and grabbed hold of the envelope and pulled it to him. "Let's see what else you lied about," Fargo said. Ralph Abel started to lunge forward. When he saw the Colt in Fargo's hand lift a half-inch, he halted.

"Bastard," Ralph Abel growled as Fargo opened the envelope and pulled out the contents, two pieces of communication, one on parchment. In fancy script, the words marched across the top of the parchment: "The Last Will and Testament of George Armor Abel," Fargo read aloud.

His eyes went to the accompanying sheet of paper, written in a scrawling, bold script. " 'Here is the will, all changed just the way you wanted. Everything goes to you now. Your uncle's signature is so good that four lawyers passed on it. One of my best jobs. I got the money you sent. Here's everything you want. Call on me anytime. Ernie D.' " Fargo finished reading aloud and fastened hard eyes on Ralph Abel. "These sure are important family papers, a doctored will with a forged signature. No wonder I didn't see any brotherly grief. He's not your brother. He's a messenger for a hired forger," Fargo said.

"You can't prove that. He won't be talking," Abel said.

"I think this letter will talk," Fargo said and glanced at the gravesite where Winifred Bivins knelt, quietly sobbing over her husband. He brought his eyes back to the others, including Melanie. She showed no remorse, only a calm defiance and he heard the incredulousness in his voice. "You were all lying. No wonder you were so concerned about finding the passengers. You had reasons, only none of them were what you said they were. Poor Winifred was the only one telling the truth." He peered at Harris and Abel. "It's over. Start filling the pits," he ordered.

"I'm taking Fred back. I'm giving him a proper burial," Winifred Bivins interrupted.

Fargo called to Ralph Abel. "Help her get the man out of there and onto her horse," he said. He stepped back and watched until the stiff body was secured to Winifred's horse. "Now you and Harris start shoveling," he said.

"I can't, not with this hand," Harris protested.

"Use your other hand. Just get at it," Fargo said coldly and stood by while the two men filled the graves. He kept one eye on the pair as he began to collect the scattered banknotes and put them into the leather briefcase. He was finished when Abel threw on the last shovelful of dirt. "Mount up. We'll be going back to town," he said and brought the Ovaro to the rear of the small band. He rode slowly as Melanie came alongside him.

"What'll happen to them?" she asked.

"They just might get a break," Fargo said.

"How?"

"The facts of life. Reality. I'll be taking the banknotes, the forged will, and the letter to the sheriff. He's a one-horse sheriff in a one-horse town. He can't up and deliver Harris and Abel all the way to Missouri or wherever. He may settle for returning the banknotes and the forged will and figure that'll be punishment enough for them."

She made no comment, riding in silence until they reached town as darkness descended. He heard the hurt and resentment in her voice. "You've no right to lump me with them," she said.

"You all lied."

"Different reasons. Theirs was greed. Mine was following through on a new life for myself. No comparing the two. You've no right," she said adamantly.

"I guess not," he conceded. "You're right. It's different with you." She gave a little snort of satisfaction as he drew up to the sheriff's office and met the sullen stares Harris and Abel gave him.

"I'm finding the doc," Harris said.

"I'm going with him," Abel added. Fargo said nothing as the two men rode off.

"What if they run?" Melanie asked.

"That'll be the sheriff's problem, not mine," Fargo said and saw something close to a sly little smile edge her lips.

"Sarah Wall is going to be at the hotel," she said. "She might welcome a visit."

"Might just do that, seeing as how I know a former friend of hers," Fargo said and she moved on looking slightly smug. He went into the sheriff's office and the lawman rose to greet him.

"You again," he said. "The last varmint you brought me is history. Wasn't much trouble getting a jury and a decision."

"This might be a little different," Fargo said and the lawman listened as he told his story. When he finished, the sheriff put everything into a sturdy safe in a corner of the office.

"You're right," he said to Fargo. "Getting all this back will be easy enough. Those two operators are a different story, but I'm sure you know that. Their crimes weren't even committed in my territory."

"They don't deserve to just walk away," Fargo said.

"What they deserve and what I can do aren't exactly the same thing," the sheriff said and Fargo's eyes conceded his words.

"You could hold them till you got a chance to ship them back," Fargo offered.

"It might be months before a territory U.S. marshal came this way. I'm not feeding them three squares a day for all that time. Besides, I'd be violating their rights and that'd backfire if they were taken back," the sheriff said. "Sometimes you have to run with what you've got and you wrecked their schemes pretty thoroughly."

"Guess so," Fargo said. He rose and left with a handshake and led the Ovaro to the hotel, where he asked for Sarah Wall. She let him in with a wide smile and a kiss but a furrow clouded her brow as he sat on the bed beside her.

"Want to tell me about it?" she said.

"About what?"

"Whatever's bothering you. It's in your eyes," she said.

He peered at her. "You're too sharp," he said. "Truth is, I'm not sure. It's over. I did my job. Yet I keep feeling it isn't. I keep feeling there's something more. It's not all in place."

"Maybe you're just still bothered by the way it all turned out, including me," she said and he allowed a rueful smile.

"That's part of it. Nobody was what they seemed to be. That keeps sticking in me. It's as if it's telling me something," he said.

"Such as?"

"I don't know, dammit," he said, frowning angrily into space. His unformed feelings stabbed at him, Melanie's words giving them a semblance of shape they hadn't had before. He was bothered by the way it had all turned out and more bothered by the shadow of things unfinished. Suddenly all the old nagging questions exploded inside him and took on shape and form. He straightened up as thoughts tumbled after each other. "It didn't fit then. It still doesn't. Maybe that's why," he said.

"What didn't fit? What are you talking about?" Melanie asked.

He stopped, realizing he was making no sense to anyone but himself. "What Collins paid me to find his stages. It never made sense. It never fit. Maybe I know why, now. The way none of you were what you seemed to be, maybe those stages of his aren't what they seem to be, either."

"A stagecoach is a stagecoach. It can't be anything else," Melanie said.

"Your concerns weren't what you said they were, none of you. Maybe his aren't, either. I thought he just didn't give a damn about the passengers. I thought he was just a callous bastard. Maybe I was wrong. Maybe there's more. I'm going to find out," Fargo said.

"How? You don't even know what to look for."

He frowned back. "Not yet," he said.

"You going to look into Collins's mind or his stagecoaches?" Melanie said and her arms came around him. "Forget it. Leave it alone."

"And keep wondering forever? No, I'm not for leaving things unfinished," Fargo said.

"All right, go get yourself killed on a crazy

hunch," Melanie said, angrily pulling away from him.

"I don't plan on that," he said quietly and pulled her back to him. "Thanks for caring." He kissed her and she refused to kiss him back. She was still frowning at him as he left the room. Outside, he walked slowly from the hotel. There were times when it was nice to have someone angry at you, he reflected. He walked through the dark night streets, the Ovaro following.

Collins had had plenty of time to reach town and put his stages away by now, Fargo mused and when he reached the man's spread he tethered the Ovaro under a shadbush and went on by himself. He circled to one side of the collection of buildings, saw there were lights on in the house, and he moved along the row of small shacks where the hands bunked. He saw only one lamp on and no one walking about and continued on to the stables. Slipping inside, he counted the horses in the stalls and came up with six. His glance went to the row of saddles hung on the wall pegs. There were only four and he grunted. Collins had paid off his extra gunslingers and sent them on their way, leaving only his usual set of hands and his backup coach horses.

He left the stable, stayed to the perimeter of the buildings, and made his way to the largest of the barns. As he drew closer, he saw the glow of light seeping out from beneath the door and he stepped to the window. Peering in, he saw no movement inside, only the lone lamp that had been left burning in one corner. Muttering a thank you, he returned to the door, edged it open, and slipped inside the large barn. Fargo saw the four Concords were near each other, but standing in sets of twos. His eyes swept the rest of the barn, saw the usual rakes, shovels, extra wagon shafts, and wooden tool boxes, all the normal elements of a storage barn. He walked to the nearest of the stage-coaches, slowly walked around it, then did the same with the second.

Melanie's accusations came back to him. He had no idea what he should be looking for. Or even if there was anything to look for. Maybe the answers lay all inside Buzz Collins. He grimaced at the thought. Yet he knew there was something, some-where, someplace. He felt it in his bones. It had changed from something that nagged at him be-cause it hadn't fit to a certainty. Except it was an uncertain certainty, he swore softly. Collins wasn't simply callous, not just selfish, not just obsessed. An obsession didn't just spring up by itself. It didn't come out of a vacuum. It had roots.

Almost abstractly, he ran his hands over the big Concord, along the weathered joistings, the smooth, sanded curves, and he bent low to exam-ine the hickory axles. He straightened up and his fingers roamed across the sides of the body where they joined the rear and front boots. He stopped, realizing that he was moving aimlessly. He swore in frustration. Had he let his imagination carry him away, he asked himself and again he rejected the thought. He was wrestling with himself when he heard the footsteps outside the door. He shot a frantic glance around the barn. The nearest and fastest hiding place was the Concord. He folded himself on the floor of the coach. But if it was the wrong one, it would be his last hiding place. He flung out a silent oath as he dashed past the stage to three barrels near the wall. The door opened as he lowered himself behind the barrels and peered out through the opening between the weathered kegs.

Buzz Collins came into the barn, closed the door behind him, and lifted the lamp. He carried it closer to the stages and set it on the floor. Next, he pulled a box over to the lamp. As Fargo watched, Buzz Collins went to the toolbox, pulled out a wrench, and walked to the right front wheel of the nearest Concord. The wrench in hand, Collins began to unscrew the hub of the wheel, loosening it first, then slowly pulling it from the axle skein. He kept slowly drawing it out until he had the thick section all the way out, far enough so he was able to slip his hand inside the space left by the tapered section of the axle. Feeling deep into the space, Collins drew his hand out finally and Fargo saw that he clutched two small burlap sacks.

Collins moved to the box with the sacks, pulled one of the sacks open, and shook the contents out onto the top of the box. Frowning in fascination as he peered between the barrels, Fargo saw the stones tumble from the sack, a small shower of color that glistened and glinted, sparkled and shimmered in the lamplight. He found himself staring in astonishment at the deep green of emerald, the blood red of ruby, the quivering yellow of topaz, the darkly mottled green of jade, and the purplish red of garnet. All the stones were polished and cut, each a precious gem of breathtaking beauty. Collins opened the second sack and another cascade of color fell onto the box top. This time Fargo recognized the purple and yellow of corundum, the swimming blue magnificence of star sapphire, the speckled black-green of black opal, and flashing with their own cold brilliance, a half-dozen ice-clear diamonds.

Collins stepped back and counted the stones. Then he picked up the wrench and carefully pushed the hub and axle back into its skein, tightened the hub, and started toward the next coach. Fargo drew his Colt and stepped out from behind the barrels. It all fit now, Collins's obsession with getting the stages back. "I've seen enough. No need to empty out the next one," he said and Collins wheeled, his jaw dropping open. He stared at Fargo, his lips quivering. "I'm sure all the others are there," Fargo said. "Poor Dockerby. He had no idea what he had. He thought he was just stealing stagecoaches. He didn't know they carried a fortune in gems."

Collins pulled his jaw closed and found his voice. "How'd you know?" he asked.

"I didn't," Fargo said. "But nothing was what it seemed to be on this job. I figured it might be the same with you. I was right."

"Son of a bitch dumb luck," Collins rasped.

"And paying attention to little things," Fargo said. "You've been smuggling precious gems I'm betting are stolen. Where do you pick them up?"

"Kansas. There's a wheelwright there. He puts them in the axle skeins," Collins said.

"For who?"

"Some gents. I don't know names. Two are Chinese," Collins said.

"Why you?" Fargo queried.

"They get the stones to Kansas but then every one of their carriers were hit. They came up with this idea and contacted me. It worked fine until Dockerby started stealing my stages, the stupid bastard," Collins grumbled.

"The gents who hired you must be very unhappy not getting their stones. I'd guess they're not buying your story about disappearing stages," Fargo said and almost smiled as alarm raced through Collins's face. "I'd even guess your time is about up," he said and again, Collins swallowed hard.

"Not now it isn't," the voice interrupted and Fargo's eyes went to the door, where he saw Leah, a Remington six-shot, single-action revolver in her hands and aimed directly at him. "Drop the gun," she said.

"Not so fast, honey," Fargo said, the Colt still trained on Collins.

"Drop it," Leah repeated.

"I press this trigger and Brother is dead," Fargo said.

"I press this trigger and the Trailsman's dead," Leah said and he swore silently. She was all too right. There was no way he could bring the Colt around quickly enough to get her. "The gun, drop it," Leah repeated, her voice hardening. Fargo's lips thinned and he swore silently. It wasn't the moment to provoke a wild showdown. He didn't feel suicidal. He lowered his arm, let the Colt drop to the floor, and heard the deep sigh of relief from Collins.

"He took me by surprise," Collins said to his sister, a whine in his voice.

"You stupid ass," Leah flung back at him, her voice made of disdain. "I told you not to go near the coaches until you were sure he'd left town. I told you you couldn't predict what he'd do."

"I thought we ought to be sure the stones were there," Collins said.

"Since when do you make decisions around here?" Leah snapped and Fargo's brows lifted as he glanced at her.

"Hold it. What happened to you never going against Buzz's decisions?" he asked.

"Shut up," Leah hissed.

"I'll be damned," Fargo said, surprise sweeping through him. "Buzz isn't in charge here. He's not in charge of shit. This is your operation."

"You won't be telling anybody," she said.

"Yes, he will," the voice cut in and Fargo's eyes went to the door again, Leah's also. Melanie was there with the Joslyn in hand and aimed at Leah. He saw Leah's gun stay trained on him.

"Join the party. You must be the little chippie he had to go rescue," Leah said calmly.

"I'm the little chippie who's going to shoot you if you don't drop the gun," Melanie said.

"Go to hell," Leah snapped and Fargo saw Melanie's eyes narrow and again he hastily cut in, afraid that one mistake could trigger a shoot-out he wanted to avoid.

"I'd listen to her," he said to Leah. "She does what she has to do, no regrets, no questions."

But Leah let a sneer cross her lips. "I don't scare," she said.

Fargo threw a glance at Buzz Collins and uttered a silent curse at what he saw. The man was on the edge, his face flushed, his tongue flicking across twitching lips. He hadn't Leah's nerves. His were already strained to the breaking point. "Everybody ease up," Fargo said calmly. He threw a quick glance at Leah and Melanie and then brought his eyes back to Buzz Collins. The man's lips continued to twitch but he remained in place and Fargo was grateful for small favors. It was Leah's voice that broke the silence as she picked up on Fargo's suggestion. For her own reasons, of course, yet she had the practical sense to back off when it was prudent. Her brother didn't and Fargo wasn't so sure Melanie did, either.

"Yes, everybody ease up," Leah echoed and cast a glance at Melanie. "You shoot, I shoot, he shoots. Everybody's dead. Nobody wins. Put down your guns and we can work out something."

"Good idea," Fargo said. "Only we start with you putting down your gun."

"Bad idea. You two first," Leah returned.

Fargo's glance went to Buzz Collins and he saw the panic sweeping the man's face, his hands trembling. Fargo threw a glance at Leah and saw that she realized how close her brother was to cracking. "Fargo's not going to shoot you, Buzz. He knows what that'll mean," she said.

"Just what it'll mean for you, bitch," Melanie said.

The wild, strangled scream came from Collins. "No . . . no more, no more," he cried out and exploded. He threw himself forward in a dive for the gun that was but a few feet from him on the floor. Everyone's eyes went to him, an automatic reaction in a moment of surprise that consumed split seconds. But Fargo already knew what the deadly chain of reaction would be. He needed no consideration, no moment of anticipation to bear fruit. He dived and hit the floor as Leah's Remington swung around and fired, her bullet hurtling over his head. He glimpsed Melanie as she fired and her shot whizzed within a fraction of an inch of Leah's shoulder.

But Buzz Collins was shooting from the floor, spraying bullets. Two of his shots hit the large kerosene lamp, the glass shattering and sending an explosion of fiery kerosene vaulting through the air in all directions. Fargo saw the flaming lines of burning kerosene smash into the walls and land on the floor of the barn. Almost as if it were paper, the tinder-dry wood of the old barn burst into flame. Instantly, the barn was afire in a dozen places at once. Fargo pulled his eyes from the eruption of flame and saw Melanie slumped against the wall, her eyes closed.

"Jesus," he heard Leah call.

"The stages," Collins shouted.

Fargo was running in a crouch toward Melanie as Leah answered. "Fuck the stages. Get out of here," she yelled and out of the corner of his eye he saw her grab Buzz by one arm. But Fargo had reached Melanie. He dropped to one knee beside her and saw the smear of blood on her temple. Leah raced from the barn, pulling her brother along with her as Fargo felt a wave of heat sweep over him from behind. He rubbed his thumb across the smear of blood and saw that it was all on the surface. The bullet had only grazed her and as he began to pull her up she opened her eyes.

"Thank God," Fargo said as Melanie's eyes regained focus and found him. Dimly, he heard the barn door slam shut and he turned, looking back across the barn. "Jesus," he breathed. In moments, the barn had become wrapped in flames. Lines of fire leaped upward along the walls in a dozen places, racing across the floor in a dozen more. He saw one of the Concords catch fire, flames leaping around each wheel to create fiery circles. "We've got to get out of here," he said to Melanie, pulling her up with him and running for the door. She was beside him as he pulled the door open and she flung herself backward with him as a hail of bullets erupted. He kicked the door shut as he hit the floor and heard the bullets thudding into the wood. "Shit," he swore as he rose, pulling Melanie with him.

He edged the door open, more carefully this time, and another hail of bullets slammed into the door. He kicked it closed again, but he had seen what he wanted to see. The bullets came from the left side and the right. Collins and Leah had positioned themselves to lay down converging lines of fire. But the fire had been too heavy for just the two of them. Collins's men were with him, taking part in the barrage. Fargo turned back to the barn as a blast of heat struck him in the face and he stared at the scene. In only minutes, the barn had become an inferno, flames leaping up all four walls to the roof and he saw another of the coaches turn into a fiery chariot.

"There's no way out," Melanie said, her voice

suddenly very small. Fargo moved forward, stepping between the trails of flame that crisscrossed the floor. The heat swept over him. The barn was fast becoming a giant oven. In another few minutes its soaring temperature would deplete the oxygen in the area. He scanned the sides, now walls of flame, and Melanie gave voice to his thoughts. "We're trapped," she said. He swore silently at the terrible truth of her words. He looked up and saw the roof was a ceiling of flame. It'd be falling pretty damn soon, he knew, his eyes moving down to sweep the inferno that had been a barn. To run out the door was to die in a hail of bullets. To stay was to burn to death or perhaps, mercifully, to die of lack of air. No choice of life or death, only the choice of how they'd prefer to die.

His eyes swept the flame-filled barn again and came to a halt, thoughts racing through his mind. The barrels he had hidden behind were still intact. They were far enough from the walls so that the flames hadn't touched them yet. "What are you thinking?" Melanie asked.

"I'm thinking you're going to roll out of here," he said. Pulling her with him, he leapfrogged over the streams of flame that ran along the floor and reached the barrels. The largest barrel held a dozen pieces of wood, but even with the wood in it there was room enough for Melanie. "Get in," he said and helped her climb into the barrel as he stomped out a tongue of flame. She dropped to her knees in the barrel as he stacked the pieces of wood around the curved sides. "This'll give you extra protection," he said.

"Where are you going to be?" she asked.

"Close. Who do you think's going to roll you out?" he said. She offered him a wry smile, more bravery than confidence in it. He knew how she felt. It was a wild chance. A bullet could go between the pieces of wood and pierce the relatively thin sides of the barrel. But a glance back at the roaring inferno, the barn almost entirely consumed by flames now, told him it was the only chance. He gripped the top edge of the barrel, pulled, and turned the barrel on its side. "Show time," he bit out grimly.

8

He danced away from a tongue of flame that licked at his feet and looked up as a section of the roof collapsed, falling in a shower of yellow-orange, burning rain. Putting his shoulder to the overturned barrel, Fargo sent it rolling over the fiery strands that crossed the floor. Digging his heels hard into the floor, he sent the barrel forward. He could feel it gather speed as it neared the door. Pushing with all his strength, ignoring the flames that grabbed at his ankles with fiery fingers, he propelled the barrel faster until it was rolling almost out of his reach. As it neared the door, he stopped pushing to leap forward and yank the door open.

Just as he did he heard the tremendous roaring sound and glanced back to see the barn roof falling in. He felt the ground shake. With a final push, he sent the barrel rolling into the open, going full speed as he stayed right behind it. The sharp sounds of gunfire cut through the crash of the roof and Fargo dropped to one knee, following the path of the bullets hitting the barrel. He spied Buzz Collins first, fired the Colt, and heard the man cry out as he went down. Fargo whirled, still on one knee, and found Leah on the other side. He saw her half turn to see her brother go down. She spun back at once, firing furiously. Fargo pitched himself forward as her shots went over his head. Shooting from on his stomach, he fired two shots and heard Leah's sharp cry of pain as she fell backward.

Turning from her, Fargo saw the barrel just as it crashed into a tree. It shattered, the staves flying off in all directions. Fargo pushed himself up and started to run forward. He stopped as he saw the figures rushing at the barrel, three of Collins's men. Guns raised to pump bullets into the figure crouched inside the barrel, the trio bore in closer. Fargo swung the Colt in a short arc as he fired and the three figures went down, almost in a row. Running forward, Fargo reached the barrel to see Melanie on her hands and knees, crawling out under the steel bands that stayed in place, holding only empty air together. He reached down and helped her out. She clung to him, drawing in deep breaths of air.

Brushing her hair back, he peered at her. There were a few streaks of red where slivers of wood had struck her but he saw that she was otherwise all right. She pulled back after a moment. "Now I know what a fish in a barrel feels like," she murmured, looking back at the column of flame that still burned furiously. He felt her shudder against him. "I'd have been in there except for you," she said.

"Leah would've shot me except for you," he said. "What made you show up?"

"You said you refused to leave things unfinished. I decided not to also." She shrugged. "Where are they? Collins and Leah?"

"I'm going to make sure. You stay here," he said, reloading the Colt as he hurried away. He sought out Buzz Collins first. He found the man's lifeless form lying facedown, his gun still clutched in one hand. Stepping past him, Fargo went on to where he'd seen Leah go down. Her short scream had been made of pain, yet it had been strong and he approached cautiously, the Colt in hand ready to fire. But he didn't see her. He frowned as he drew closer to the area and halted when he saw where she had been. The bloodstains were fresh, of course, but wide, and he saw where she had pulled herself up. The trail led to the house and he followed, in through the still open front door and down the hallway.

It led into a study, a desk and chairs to one side, and then he saw her, on the floor in front of an open safe. A roll of bills lay on the floor and Leah pulled herself around, the Remington in one hand, the roll of bills under her other hand. The red stain covered the entire front of her blouse. "Bastard," she hissed. The revolver waved as she tried to bring it up. A red smear on her pale white skin made it look redder than it was.

"Put the gun down. I'll get a doctor," Fargo said.

She cursed again at him, her voice hardly audible this time. He stepped to one side as she tried to bring the Remington up again. Once more, the revolver swayed. He started to back out of the room and run for a doctor when he heard the hollow sigh, then the terrible rattle that came from her throat. The gun fell from her hand and Leah's head dropped onto her red-stained chest. Her other hand stayed clutching the roll of bills. Life, always choosing its own time and place, had chosen that moment to leave her. He felt the deep sigh escape his lips and wanted to feel sorry for her. But he realized he couldn't. She had used beauty to mask cold greed, deception to hide utter selfishness, she had used everything and everyone, including her poor, weak brother. Holstering the Colt, he turned his back on Leah Collins and hurried from the house. She'd been one more thing that wasn't what it seemed to be.

He reached Melanie and saw the questions in her eyes. "It's over," he said.

"I thought that once before," she said.

"This time it is," he said. Melanie cast a glance at the barn, now a collapsed heap of smoking, still smoldering rubble.

"What about the stones?" she asked.

"They could withstand the fire. They're all that could. Maybe somebody will find them when the ashes cool. Maybe not," Fargo said. "You want to wait around?"

"No," she said firmly, shaking her head. "I don't care what they might be worth. I just want to leave here. I don't even want to stay at the hotel."

Fargo saw people coming, drawn by the fire, townsfolk gathering to stare curiously at the scene. Somebody would put it all together come morning, the sheriff, probably. Fargo circled to the side, leaving Melanie in the trees as he got the horses and returned with them. He waited at the hotel as Melanie got her things and rode close beside him as he led the way out of town. He left the road a half mile or so on and rode into the low hills, where he found a glen of silver fir on the other side of an open plateau. He unsaddled the horses, set out his bedroll, undressed, and slid into it. Melanie came in beside him, her beautifully high, firm breasts pressing warmly into his chest.

"Just hold me," she said and he nodded, understanding the inner turmoil that still raged inside her. She clung to him and he joined her in sleep as the moon crossed the midnight sky. He slept deeply, his body making its own demands and he was still hard asleep when the dawn crept its way across the land. Yet he was not totally exhausted and that's what it took to close down that part of him that could hear the sounds only the lynx and mountain lion could hear, to still that special inner sense only the wild creatures possessed.

He heard the soft, scraping sound, boots against loose soil. His hand slowly moved to the Colt lying at his side, stopped, and found itself touching the warm softness of Melanie's breast. He swore silently. As she had turned in the night she'd pushed aside his holster. He drew his hand back. The soft, scraping sound had stopped and the voice took its place. "Well now, this is right cozy," it said. Fargo slowly turned and saw the figure standing in front of him, the square head and long sideburns peering at him with a sneer. "Real little turtledoves, aren't you?" Rod Harris said. Fargo looked at the six-gun in the man's hand, a Smith & Wesson five-shot, single-action piece. Another sound came, this one from behind him, and he turned to see Ralph Abel, gun in hand.

Melanie took that moment to wake. She sat up and blinked, seeing Rod Harris. She grabbed at the edge of the sleeping bag and pulled it up to cover her breasts. "Real nice, but we've other things in mind," Harris said, motioning to Fargo with his gun. "Get up and get dressed," he said. Melanie took the opportunity to pull on clothes as Fargo stood up and dressed. When he finished, he shot a glance at both men. They had him sandwiched. He measured the distance to the Colt on the ground in its holster. He might, with luck, reach it quickly enough to get one of the two men. But never both. Or one might shoot and miss but not both.

"Get away from the gun," Harris said as if picking up his thoughts. "We've got your rifle too." Fargo moved away from the Colt and Ralph Abel came closer.

"You're going to get us our things back," he said.

"What?" Fargo frowned.

"Our things. Rod's banknotes and the will for me," Ralph Abel said.

"I can't do that. It's all in the sheriff's hands," Fargo said.

"Then you get it out of his hands," Harris said.

"I can't do that. He wouldn't go along with that," Fargo said.

"Then make him," Harris returned and stepped over to Melanie. With startling suddenness he sank a punch into her midsection. She went down onto her hands and knees with a gasp of pain.

Fargo started for Harris, but stopped as the man's gun rose up. "She's as good as dead unless you bring those bearer notes back to me," Harris said. "We'll be taking her with us. You get her back when you bring me the notes and Abel the will."

"This is crazy. I can't do it. The sheriff won't go along with it, I tell you," Fargo insisted.

"Sweet-talk him, convince him, or shoot him. We don't care. No banknotes, no will, she's dead," Harris said.

"How do I find you?" Fargo asked.

"You just show up right here," Abel said. Harris reached down and pulled Melanie up by her hair and she cried out in pain.

"I'd get my ass moving if I were you, Fargo," the man said. Fargo, his lips a thin line, went to the Ovaro, saddled the horse, and met Harris's icy stare. "Don't even think about bringing a posse back with you. We'll be watching. Anyone but you even shows, she's dead. Don't come back wearing a gun, either." Fargo wheeled the horse around. "And I want every goddamn one of those bearer bonds back. If there's even one missing, she's dead." Fargo found Melanie's eyes, saw the fear and pain in them, sent her a silent message of confidence, and put the pinto into a trot.

He rode away, his lips drawn back in helpless fury. He wanted to turn into the trees at the bottom of the plateau and make his way back and get both Harris and Abel. But without a gun he knew it'd be a slender thread of a chance. He had no doubt that Harris would kill Melanie. It had been in the man's eyes, the implacable coldness of a man playing his last card. Fargo's mind raced as

144

he rode and he found himself quickly discarding one plan after another to get at Harris and Abel. He swore in frustration as each fell apart, each foundering on the one most important element, Melanie's life.

Harris had dealt himself the top hand and Fargo had to concede that there was no answer except to obey the man's orders. But the closer he came to Bolton Flats the more he realized that might not be so easy. No sheriff would simply hand back a small fortune in possibly stolen banknotes. It would not only violate his oath of office and be contrary to everything he stood for, but it would make him an accomplice to a crime. Humane reasons notwithstanding, it could end his career. Rod Harris's words swam into Fargo's thoughts. *Sweet-talk him, convince him, or shoot him.* It was an order he didn't want to think of following, a scenario he didn't want to see played out. Somehow, he'd have to make the first two parts work. He'd have to convince the lawman that with the banknotes he could not only save Melanie's life but get the notes back.

Fargo groaned and wondered how he could manage any of it when he couldn't be sure of the first, must less the second. The town came into sight and Fargo didn't slow the pinto as he skirted wagons and weaved his way through the main street. Skidding to a halt outside the sheriff's office, he strode in to see a thin, balding man with a dour face sitting at the desk. "Who're you?" Fargo barked.

"Deputy Akers," the man said.

"Where's the sheriff?" Fargo asked.

"Gone," the man said.

"What do you mean, gone?" Fargo frowned.

"Gone. Vamoosed. Quit," the deputy said. Fargo felt as though he'd been kicked in the stomach by a mule as he stared at the man.

"No. That can't be," he muttered.

"Guess again, mister. Who are you?" Deputy Akers said.

"Skye Fargo. I had some business with the sheriff," Fargo answered.

"Yes, he said you might be back," the deputy said and reached into a draw, pulled out a large envelope and tossed it on the desk. "He left this for you," Akers said.

Fargo opened the envelope. The first thing that tumbled from it was the forged will. Next came a smaller piece of paper that Fargo unfolded. He stared down at the few lines on it.

"Do whatever you want with the will. The banknotes were bearer bonds. Anybody can cash them. All that money is more than I'd make in a lifetime on this stinking job. Decided to cash the bonds in myself. Adios Amigos."

Fargo stared at the note, thoughts a wild carousel in his head, curses a torrent on his tongue. There'd be no need to convince the good sheriff of anything, no need to bargain, to plead, to promise. Everything had blown up in his face. One thought stood out from all the others, vibrating in its terrible irony. It fitted. In its own terrible, tragic, perverse way, it fitted. Mourners who were not what they seemed to be, stagecoaches that

146

were more than they seemed to be, and now a sheriff who was not what he ought to be. It fitted everything else about this place, this job. Fargo's eyes went to the deputy.

"You know where he went?" Fargo asked.

"Nope. Nobody does. He just turned in his badge and left," the deputy said.

"No family, girlfriend, nobody he'd talk to?"

"No. The sheriff was always a loner."

"Goddamn," Fargo bit out as he strode from the office. He had come there with only a slim hope and now there was nothing. What little chance there had been left was now gone, shattered into a thousand pieces. The man's corrupt, selfish act had sealed Melanie's death. Going back to Harris with the truth would be a waste of time. Harris would never believe him, never. Fargo walked down the street, a man in shocked helplessness as the Ovaro followed obediently. People, wagons, buildings were only shapes, abstract forms, a blur of gray when suddenly he stopped and stared, sudden excitement spiraling through him. The word over the doorway of the brick building on the corner exploded in front of him: BANK.

Thoughts cascaded through Fargo's mind. The bearer bonds were cashable anywhere, guaranteed by the maker. But a strange bank might hesitate, ask for more information, identity. Cashing them at a bank where he was known would have been the logical and easy way to go. Fargo erupted in a dash across the street. He burst into the bank and found a young man wearing a teller's viser who looked up, startled. "Who's in charge here?" Fargo shot at him.

"Our president, Mr. Murphy," the youth said.

"Get him," Fargo almost roared and the young man disappeared. He returned in moments with a portly ruddy-faced man with gray hair and clothed in a banker's frock coat.

"You asked to see me, mister?" the banker said.

"The sheriff, was he here, maybe yesterday, maybe the day before?" Fargo questioned.

"Yes, he was," the man said.

"He cashed in a small fortune in bearer bonds," Fargo said.

"Yes. He said it was official business," the banker answered. "Who might you be, mister?"

"Name's Fargo. I gave him those notes. He was supposed to send them back to the maker. He didn't. You cashed them and he skipped out," Fargo said.

The banker stared back, his mouth hanging open. Finally, he pulled it closed. "My God. Is this true?" he murmured.

"True as the nose on your face," Fargo bit out.

"This is terrible. It's a breach of his office," the banker said.

"I don't think he cared much about that," Fargo said and saw the banker draw himself up pompously.

"Look here, this may be a terrible thing but I acted perfectly properly. I did nothing wrong in cashing those bearer bonds," he said.

"Didn't say you did," Fargo answered. "But because of what's happened, a girl's life is at stake."

"How unfortunate but I don't see how that involves me," Murphy said.

"You cashed the notes. That involved you. I don't get those notes back, she dies," Fargo said.

The banker frowned. "They've been cashed. I can't give them back."

"Call it a loan," Fargo said.

"That's preposterous," the man snapped.

"You'll get them back," Fargo tried and felt his patience dwindling.

"I suppose you'll guarantee that with collateral," the banker said, a sneer in his tone.

"I'll guarantee a lot more if you don't give them to me," Fargo said, his voice hardening.

Murphy swallowed. "I can't, even if I wanted to," he said.

"Give me a reason and it better be a good one," Fargo said.

"They've already been mailed to the maker, a bank in Kansas, if I recall correctly. We send such bonds out the minute they're cashed and we're reimbursed upon receipt," the banker said.

"Shit," Fargo swore and his lips pulled back in a grimace. His thoughts raced and he bit out the word. "Cash," he said. Harris would take cash. "Give me the amount of the bonds in cash," he told Murphy.

An expression of horror crossed the man's ruddy face. "Ridiculous. You want me to pay them again?" he said.

"And be quick about it," Fargo snapped.

"I won't do any such thing. My board of directors would have my head," the man said.

Fargo drew the Colt. "They can bury all of you, not just your head if you don't," he said. "Start filling a sack."

"You're being the same as a bank robber," Murphy protested.

"It's in a good cause," Fargo said and pulled back the hammer on the Colt, let it click loudly in the small room. The banker's face lost its ruddiness. "Let's go. Get that vault open. You too," Fargo said to the young teller. He locked the front door behind him and followed the two men into the rear room of the bank where Murphy knelt down in front of a heavy safe. The teller brought out a canvas sack and set it on the floor as the safe door opened. "Big bills. I want to be able to carry it," Fargo said and watched as both men began putting money into the sack. "All the notes. No short-changing," Fargo warned, keeping the Colt trained on both men as they stuffed the sack with bills. When they finished, the teller knotted the top of the sack closed. The Colt still in his hand, Fargo swung the sack over his shoulder. "You'll be glad you did this," he said to Murphy.

"You'll be sorry," the banker said.

"Call the sheriff," Fargo threw back as he ran out the door and climbed onto the Ovaro.

9

He rode from town, the canvas sack tied to the saddle horn and the grim reality stabbed at him as he rode. He had the money. He could go to Harris. There was suddenly a chance for Melanie. But he had no plan to make that chance happen. Just turning the money over to Harris wouldn't guarantee Melanie's life. He couldn't trust Harris to keep his word. In fact, there was little chance that he would. Everyone who knew about him would be a constant threat, somewhere, sometime. Harris would live a lot more comfortably if Melanie no longer existed.

Fargo's mouth was a thin line and he slowed the horse. He needed time to put together a plan. All he had right now was that Harris and Abel were ready and waiting. Turning the money over to them was growing less and less attractive. He'd use it as a last resort if he couldn't come up with something better. The two men took shape in his mind. They had put their heads together for their mutual good, their mutual self-interest. But they were not friends. They had no ties to one another. Fargo's eyes grew narrow in thought and he let the pieces come together in his mind. His best chance was to play Abel and Harris against each other. It would be not unlike walking a high-wire tightrope. One misstep and it would be over for him. And for Melanie, he added grimly. Yet once again he had no choice.

When he reached the plateau he didn't cross it but turned into the forest of hackberry that bordered the plateau. He carefully made his way through the trees until he neared the end and the forest of silver fir. He tied the pinto to a branch and went on foot, circling through the firs until he reached the glen. He stepped forward and walked carefully, aware of the ominous silence. The figure stepped into view, Ralph Abel, gun in hand. "Where's your horse?" the man asked nervously.

"Back a ways," Fargo said.

"You dumb enough to bring a posse?" Abel questioned.

"You see anybody?" Fargo returned.

"I don't see you carrying anything, either," Abel growled.

Fargo slowly reached into his pocket and drew out the will and handed it to the man. He saw Abel's eyes light up as he glanced at the document. "The banknotes?" Abel asked, pushing the will into his pocket.

"I've got better," Fargo said. "Cash."

Abel's eyes narrowed. "Cash?" he echoed and Fargo nodded. "Where?" Abel asked.

"With my horse," Fargo said.

"You playing games?" Abel queried.

"No games," Fargo said.

"It'd be a mistake. Harris is waiting," the man growled.

"I want Melanie alive," Fargo said. "You help

me get Harris and there's a helluva lot of money waiting for you, ten times more than you'll get with that will." Abel peered at him but Fargo saw the tiny lights forming in the man's eyes. Abel was on the hook and Fargo slid a step closer. "You help me. I'll help you," he said. Abel's brow furrowed in thought.

"How do I know you're not lying? I want to see that cash," the man said. Fargo shrugged nonchalantly. He had tried to avoid that question but he had expected it.

"Wait here," he said. He hurried away, knowing that the man's gun stayed on him till he was out of sight. When he returned on the Ovaro he had the sack in one hand. He dropped it to the ground in front of Abel, who undid the top immediately. Fargo saw his eyes grow wide as he stared at the sack of bills. "It can be all yours," Fargo said and stepped closer to Abel. "I get Melanie, take care of Harris, and you're home free." The seed had blossomed into a tree, Fargo saw, the face of opportunity and greed taking over Abel's every feature. Fargo moved another step closer and stopped as Abel suddenly looked up at him.

"I could shoot you, take the money, and run," he said.

"And have Harris after you the rest of your life?" Fargo said. Abel frowned. "My way I take care of him and you're gone."

"All right," Abel said, lowering the gun.

"Where has he got Melanie?" Fargo asked and took another step closer.

"Quarter mile straight north, a hollow of lodgepole pine. I don't check in every hour, she's dead," Abel said.

"How much time's left?" Fargo frowned.

"Fifteen minutes," the man said. Fargo nodded and smiled. His fist, when it shot out, snapped forward as though it were a diamondback striking. The blow caught Abel on the point of the chin and he went flying backward, hitting the ground. He tried to get up when Fargo's next blow, a short, chopping left, smashed him down again. He lay half conscious, breathing hard. Fargo scooped up his gun and started to push it into his holster, then took it out, emptied the bullets from it, and threw it into the trees. Harris would be looking for a gun on him. He couldn't take the chance he'd find it, Fargo decided.

Abel came fully conscious as Fargo was finishing the last knot in the lariat that bound him head and foot. "You bastard," Abel spit out. "You stinkin', rotten bastard."

"Greed is a terrible thing," Fargo said as he stuffed a gag into Abel's mouth. He secured it with a kerchief and dragged the man deep into the trees. He bound him tightly to one of the young firs and hurried away. Returning the sack to the saddle horn, he rode north, slowing when he spied the first lodgepole pine. He went on another dozen yards and dismounted. Hiding the Ovaro in a dense thicket, he moved forward on foot, pausing only to draw the thin throwing knife from its calf holster. He pushed the blade inside his shirt and kept it in place by securing the tip inside his waist. He moved at a crouch, slowing as he came to a cleared spot, where he saw Rod Harris, six-gun in hand.

Frowning, he scanned the trees and it took him a moment to find Melanie hanging in the air on one of the tall, thin pines that were clustered together. A rope was loose around her neck, running down to where Harris sat on a log. Fargo saw the knife lying beside him and looked up again at the contraption that had been rigged up for Melanie. One slice of the knife would sever the rope. It would also send Melanie, her body acting as a counterweight, plunging downward, breaking her neck in moments. Fargo cursed at Harris's macabre cleverness. The man could sever the rope in an instant and once the rope was cut Melanie was dead. Even if he got close enough, Fargo saw, he could never grab hold of the severed rope in time to prevent Melanie's plunge downward.

Somehow he had to keep Harris from cutting the rope. He thought about changing his plan and decided against it. He had nothing better and the first half had worked. He stepped forward, into the open where Harris could see him. Harris had his gun up and aimed instantly, letting his eyes look up at Melanie. She saw him and let hope come into her eyes. Harris glanced past him, a frown coming over his face. "Where's Abel?" Harris asked.

Fargo let a wry snort escape his lips. "Your friend Abel?" he said. "He's gone."

Harris took a step toward him and cocked the six-gun menacingly. "What do you mean gone?"

"Gone, as in run away," Fargo said.

"You're lying," Harris said and took a step back

toward the stump with the knife on it. "You're lying and she's dead."

"You don't see him, do you?" Fargo said.

"You got to him," Harris said. "Where are the banknotes?"

"The sheriff sent them back. I brought cash," Fargo said, choosing his words carefully. This was the moment he had to do with Harris what he'd done with Abel, play them against each other and feed on their petty suspicions. "Your friend Abel took the cash from me. Then he saw how much goddamn money it was, ten times what that phoney Will would get him. I thought he was going to bring it to you but he kept the gun on me, took the sack, and high-tailed it," Fargo said, keeping his voice matter-of-fact.

"I don't believe you," Harris said and Fargo swore silently. Harris didn't have trust. He was just more suspicious. "I told you, no games or she's dead." Harris snarled.

"Didn't come to play games. Came to make a deal," Fargo said. Harris peered hard at him but waited. "I know which way he went. I can find him," Fargo said.

"Not without me." Harris growled. Fargo almost smiled. It was working.

"Fair enough. Let her down and I'll find him with you." Harris still waited, wrestling with his suspicions and his fears. Fargo felt the tiny beads of perspiration on his hands. This was the moment of truth, the crucial seconds that would tell him if his plan had worked twice. "Every minute you waste he's getting further away with your money," Fargo said. "Let her down and we'll still get him."

Harris held on to his canniness. "We find him. Then I'll come back and let her down," he said and Fargo swore inwardly. It was not the response he expected or wanted, but did he dare risk a worse one? The man's one hand was inches from the knife on the stump, the other holding the gun on him. The tightrope was almost at an end. But he had to make one more effort.

"Let her down first. Something might happen while we're chasing Abel," he said.

Harris's strained inner tensions exploded. "No, goddammit," he shouted and his hand closed around the knife beside the rope. "My way or she's dead."

Fargo raised his hands placatingly and took a step backward. "All right, you win. We do it your way," he said. He waited till Harris took his hand from the knife on the stump. He shot a glance at Melanie, saw the helpless fear in her round eyes. "You want to get your horse first?" he asked the man.

"Goddamn right I do," Harris said and started toward his mount. Fargo's quick glance told him he was less than six feet from the rope that still held Melanie in place. His hand stole into the front of his shirt, closed around the hilt of the throwing knife against his chest when Harris suddenly whirled. "No, goddammit, I don't like it. Something's wrong. I feel it in my bones," the man shouted, all his distrust, suspicion, and fear exploding inside him. But the gun was still held low at the end of his arm, still pointed downward.

157

The moment had exploded in his face, Fargo knew. There'd be no other.

He drew the throwing knife, used a wrist motion and sent the thin, double-edged blade hurtling through the air. Harris's eyes widened as he saw the blade coming at him. He tried to duck away and bring his gun up at the same time and lost precious moments trying. The long, slender blade plunged deep into his abdomen but Fargo saw his gun fire, saw where the barrel was pointed. Fargo was spinning, diving, and throwing himself into the air as the man's shot hit the knot holding the rope that ran up to Melanie. Reaching out as far as he could with both hands, he managed to curl his fingers around the rope as it tore loose.

He hung on, his weight taking the place of the knot that held the rope down but he saw Melanie's body drop an inch, the rope tightening around her neck. He swung at the end of the rope and used his legs to keep swinging, remembering how he used to swing as a child. But there was no way he could reach the place where it had been knotted. Even trying would loosen the rope enough to plunge Melanie downward and to a broken neck. Cursing, he kept swinging. Harris was on the ground, legs drawn up, the knife in his midsection. Using the leverage of the swinging rope and the added push of his legs, he swung close enough to one of the pines to hit it with his feet. With the added momentum, he was able to increase his swings and he bounced himself off another tree and went back to the first, until he was swinging back and forth with real force. Tensing his every muscle, he measured the last swing and as he hurtled toward the opposite tree, he braced himself, drew his legs up, and let his body slam into the tree.

The shock went through him, a flash of shuddering pain, as he wrapped his arms around the tree trunk, hung for a moment, and flung the rope around the nearest branch. Clinging to the rope, he pulled it tight around the branch, and held it in place until he regained enough strength to wrap another circle in the rope. Assured that it was tight enough to hold, he pulled himself onto the adjoining branch and tied a knot in the rope. He rested and felt his muscles quivering, his body still reacting to the shock of colliding with the tree. He lifted his head and peering up at Melanie, he saw the hope mixed with relief in her face. He nodded at her, pulled himself up, and began to climb up the branches of the thin tree until he reached her.

"We've got to find a better place to meet," he said.

"I'm all for that," she said. He reached over, slipped the rope from around her neck and tossed it aside. He helped her lean out to the branch and pull herself over.

"Start climbing down," he said and began to lower himself from branch to branch, watching her as she followed with both caution and determination. Reaching the ground, he caught her and swung her down and she clung to him for a long moment. "Get your horse," he said as he stepped over to Harris. He took back his Colt, knife and from the man's horse, his rifle. "We've one more stop on the way to town," he said, and Melanie followed him as he walked back to where he'd left the Ovaro, then returned to where Abel was bound and gagged in the thicket. He freed the man, pulled the will from his pocket, and tore it into little pieces and threw it to the winds as Abel glowered. "Where there's no will there's no way," he said. "Don't come back, ever."

The man almost fell in his haste to climb onto his horse and raced away. Fargo took the Ovaro and rode back to Bolton Flats with Melanie. She went into the bank with him as he tossed the canvas sack on the floor in front of the banker. "I never expected this," the banker said in astonishment.

"That's the way of things around here. Nothing is what it seems to be," Fargo said and saw Melanie smile. She walked from the bank holding his arm and he rode south until nightfall, when he found a spot in an arbor of peach life willows near a stream. She came to him in all her young, high-breasted vibrant loveliness and when her cries of pleasure finally died away, she lay half over him, a tiny smile playing across her round-cheeked face.

"Sarah Wall's never been made love to before," she said. "That shows you."

"Shows you what?" He frowned.

She moved and pressed her soft, warm, moist portal to him. "Some things are always what they seem to be," she murmured.

"Thank God for that," he said and let flesh agree with words.

LOOKING FORWARD!
The following is the opening
section from the next novel in the exciting
Trailsman **series from Signet:**

THE TRAILSMAN #195
Fort Ravage Conspiracy

1860, in the Nevada desert
where and isolated army outpost
is called Fort Ravage
because nobody comes back alive . . .

Colonel Benjamin Colfax scanned the six soldiers as they lined up by twos beside their horses inside the huge gate of the adobe fort. The harsh morning light promised a scorching day to come. The soldiers were a motley handful, unshaven, shirttails out, uniforms filthy, and boots caked with dust. Their horses were dull with dirt and sweat and the saddles hadn't been oiled for a long time. To a man, all six soldiers returned his gaze defiantly. And with more than defiance—in their eyes was a secretive hatred, a twisted anger. The colonel knew every single soldier under his command wanted him dead.

"Major Roland, come forward," the colonel

called out. He tried to keep the bitterness out of his voice, the anger that all his efforts at discipline had failed. He tried to stay professional and cool. But he knew the soldiers heard his frustration and even took delight in it.

Major Roland moved his horse forward a step and doffed his battered hat insolently, rubbing his sweaty face burned carmine by the sun. The major's gut draped over his belt and his shirt was unbuttoned. A long diagonal scar cut across his hairy stomach, which had given him the nickname Major Scarbelly. Scarbelly didn't bother to salute, but nodded to his superior and then belched. The soldiers exchanged smirks. Colonel Colfax gritted his teeth and ignored the effrontery.

"Major Roland," he snapped. "Call for the mount."

"Prepare to mount," Scarbelly said in a snide voice.

The soldiers didn't wait for the order, but began clambering onto their horses. With a groan, Scarbelly hoisted himself onto his swaybacked chestnut and never bothered to give the official command.

Colonel Benjamin Colfax turned away in disgust. He inserted the toe of his spit-polished boot into his stirrup and swung himself up onto his gleaming gray. He was well aware how he looked in the eyes of the men. He sat tall on his horse, his wool sack coat with its single row of brass eagle buttons and gold epaulets glimmering in the sun, his blond hair and mustache trimmed neatly, the long blue barrels of his pistols burnished to a high sheen. Yes, damn it, he thought. Pride was part of army discipline. Part of what made a fighting force hold together in the bad times.

"You fellows have yourself a good time out there," one of the soldiers milling around inside the fort called out.

"Don't you boys get lost," another added.

Colonel Colfax glanced toward a group of soldiers lounging around and playing cards in the shade of the tall adobe wall that surrounded Fort Ravage. They were as sloppy as the six he was about to lead out on patrol, some of them barefoot and shirtless, their pistols jammed into leather belts. The soldiers would spend the day aimlessly, playing cards, gambling, getting into fights among themselves. A few would keep a desultory look out from the top of the wall.

It was a helluva way to run a U.S. Army outpost, Colonel Colfax thought. The moment he arrived at Fort Ravage, a month ago, he'd seen that the army discipline had completely broken down. And like any good soldier, his instinct had been to reestablish order. But at every turn, he'd been opposed by the general. The general. He gritted his teeth at the thought of him. And very quickly he'd realized discipline was beside the point—he'd had his hands full just staying alive.

The wide wooden gates began to swing slowly open to reveal the shimmering land of rocks and sand and alkali. Far in the distance were a few jagged buttes and then the endless cloudless sky already fading to white in the gathering heat of the day. The colonel brought his gray around to ride out.

"Go get us some hostiles!" a soldier called out.

"Bring us back a few of them red scalps."

"How 'bout a fresh colonel's scalp?" The voice was close at hand, but spoke in an undertone—the colonel knew it was one of the six men he was about to ride out with. It didn't matter which one. As far as he could tell, every man in Fort Ravage was trying to kill him. But then, he had known that was going to be the case when he took on this assignment. He pretended not to have heard the remark.

"Fall in," Colfax snapped, not waiting for Major Scarbelly to give the order.

A flicker of motion caught his eye and he saw the dim outline of the general standing in the window of the command hut. Out of long habit, Colonel Colfax saluted smartly as he rode past, but the general only watched, slack-eyed, then raised the half-empty bottle of whiskey to his mouth and turned away.

Colonel Colfax rode out of the gate of Fort Ravage and as he passed beyond the adobe walls, he could feel the vastness of the land take hold of him, its sandy emptiness stretching far to the horizon. Somewhere out in the desert were marauding Paiutes. That's what the general had told him. That's what was written into the official reports sent by courier weekly to army headquarters in Fort Independence. And along with the courier went the colonel's special coded message. So far there had been hardly anything to report. Colonel

Colfax hadn't seen a shred of evidence of a Paiute uprising anywhere in the territory. In fact, he hadn't spotted a live Indian during the entire month. Just to break the tedium, Colonel Colfax himself had instituted regular inspection patrols. Every other day he took a small unit out on patrol and he spotted signs of Paiutes in the area—abandoned campfires, game trails, occasional lost arrows stuck in the sands. But wherever the hostiles were, they were keeping well out of sight.

What Colonel Colfax had seen were a lot of mysterious comings and goings in Fort Ravage itself, soldiers disappearing on unexplained five-day inspection details, and animated conversations that suddenly halted as soon as he approached. When he'd questioned the general about the so-called inspection details, he'd gotten only stony silence in reply. Colfax was certain that the mysterious inspections were connected to the reason he'd been sent to Fort Ravage. And he wrote that in the special coded reports that he sent back to headquarters with the courier, messages that would seem innocuous to a casual reader. But he was also sure that wherever the soldiers were going had to do with the reason everybody at Fort Ravage seemed intent on killing him. He had no doubt the general was part of it too.

In the past month, they'd tried to get rid of him several times. First were the scorpions that found their way into his boots every morning. One bite and he'd have been paralyzed a few days, two and he'd have been a dead man. But he'd done desert duty before and he'd always been in the habit of shaking out his boots and his clothing before getting dressed each morning. Then the rattlesnake appeared in his bed one night. He'd been lucky it had moved under the covers, stirring just before he slipped into his cot. He'd killed it with one blow of his pistol butt, then tossed it out into the yard. Next a heavy crate had fallen off the wall one day as he was walking through the yard, missing him by inches. Then a barrel of gunpowder suddenly blew up as he was taking inventory of the ordnance supplies. That time he'd escaped by pure chance, having accidentally stumbled backward and fallen behind a pile of cannonballs that sheltered him from the blast and the flames. None of these occurrences were accidents. Each one had been intended to kill him. But how much longer would his luck hold out? Long enough for him to find out what he needed to know?

They rode four hours through the deserted land. Today there were no fresh signs of Paiutes. Mile after mile, the scruffy sage gave way to alkali flats, then to broken rocks, then gray sage again. The sun was a white-hot disc in the sky and sweat trickled down the colonel's face.

When they had almost reached the southernmost boundary of the land they were supposed to patrol each day, Colonel Colfax decided to call a halt. He led the way along the edge of a long ridge of red rocks, like the spine of a dragon. Just ahead, the line of rocks came to an end and ahead lay a sun-baked mudflat that became a water hole during the rainy season. The skeletons of a few dead trees rose in the distance. There was a small spot of shade to the side of one of the rocks, large enough to cool a few of the horses at a time. It was as good a place to stop as any.

"Give the order for a halt," said Colfax to Major Scarbelly, "just ahead here." Colfax turned half about in his saddle to look back at the straggling line of soldiers behind him. In answer, Scarbelly slumped down in his saddle and his eyes narrowed as he nodded to his commanding officer.

Colfax didn't like Scarbelly's expression and he felt a twitch between his shoulder blades as he turned about-face forward again. They might just shoot him in the back. If all the men at Fort Ravage and the general as well wanted him dead, then what was to prevent them from just murdering him right here, right now, in cold blood? They would send word back to army headquarters that the Paiutes did it. And there would be nobody to say different. They didn't even need to make it look like an accident.

Colonel Colfax felt the wariness grow in him as they approached the stopping point. His instincts had always been good. From his many years in command, he'd learned to read men, could feel what they were thinking. There was something in the air now, a kind of gathering tension, like before a thunderstorm.

"You mean stop right here?" Scarbelly asked laconically. The colonel hesitated for a moment, wondering if he should change his mind and insist they ride on. But that wouldn't make him any safer. No, it was better to be on guard but not let them know it. He nodded. "Company halt," Scarbelly yelled out.

"Quarter hour rest," Colonel Colfax said, dismounting. As the men got down from their horses, opened their canteens, and watered their horses, the colonel busied himself with his horse as he observed them surreptitiously. He saw them nodding to one another, exchanging glances. Scarbelly was smirking. Yeah, this was it. The game was up. Should he ride out now? Or take them all on? He rested his hand on the butt of his pistol and leaned against the flank of his tall gray for a moment, considering his options.

Suddenly, he heard a faint noise. A cry of some kind. From some distance away. Colonel Colfax raised his head and turned it to hear better, listening, listening. Yes, there it was again. He hesitated and then curiosity overcame caution. He stepped out onto the cracked mudflat, listening, following the faint cry. The dry wind carried the sound. Behind him, the men fell silent as they watched him, wondering what was going on. The colonel shaded his eyes and peered through the rising waves of heat, scanning the horizon, the black naked trees that wavered in the distance. He pulled out his small brass telescope and swept the landscape. There. He spotted it.

"My God," he muttered. "My God."

The sight was unbelievable, like something from a nightmare. He wasn't sure he was seeing what he was seeing. He became aware of the men walking up behind him but the danger had dissipated, at least temporarily, as the soldiers gathered uneasily, peering into the distance. The colonel handed the telescope to the soldier who had come up next to him.

"Jesus," the man said when he'd looked through it. Wordlessly, he handed it on. The other soldiers took a look. In one of the distant trees hung some kind of a cage. And in it was the form of a human.

"Hey! Maybe it's one of them Paiutes and we can have us some fun," Scarbelly said, breaking the shocked silence. "Let's go have a look." Several of the men raced toward their horses.

"Wait," said Colonel Colfax in such a commanding voice that the normally rebellious men stopped in their tracks. "It might well be a trap. We're going in on full alert."

And for once, the men were cooperative as he gave the orders. Two men stayed far back in a rear guard, rifles at the ready, to watch the rocks in case an ambush came from that direction. Two others rode out toward the tree and took positions far out on either side as lookouts. Major Scarbelly and a recruit named Bucknell rode forward with Colonel Colfax as they crossed the barren flat and approached.

The scene grew more horrible the closer they came—the caged man hanging in the ravaged tree. All around the tree lay slaughtered animals—the remains of a cougar and a bristly peccary that had been hacked apart and staked to the ground. Vultures picked at the bits of tattered skin and the bones. The ragged birds flew up in a dusty scattering of wings at their advance. Strange signs in colored chalks were drawn on the ground around a black firepit.

Colonel Colfax raised his eyes to the square cage made of stout branches lashed together. Inside, the powerfully built man stood stripped to the waist, his face and body and dark hair smeared with what looked like dried blood and dirt. He was bearded, not a Paiute. His eyes were wild and his hands were bound behind him and to a bar of the cage to hold him half upright. His lips were cracked and bleeding.

"Wa—ter," the man rasped. "Give—me." Colonel Colfax glanced around behind him and got the all-clear signal from the distant lookouts.

"Private Bucknell, get the man some water," Colfax commanded. The private rode forward until he came up to the cage, which hung a good five feet off the ground. Bucknell seemed confused about what to do. "Stand on your saddle and cut his hands free. Now," Colfax snapped.

Bucknell did as he was told, sawing through the rawhide that held the man's arms to the cage. The imprisoned man staggered as his hands came free and the cage creaked and swung back and forth. The prisoner rubbed his wrists and then took the canteen that was handed up to him between the wooden bars. He drank long and gratefully, then dashed some of the remaining water over his face and rubbed it.

Colonel Colfax felt a wave of surprise come over him as the grime was washed from the man's face. Astonishment swept through him as he recognized the features.

"Fargo?" he called out. *"Skye Fargo?"*

The man in the cage scarcely took notice, but rubbed his face with one hand and signaled impatiently for the private to hand him another canteen.

"Fargo? Skye Fargo? Is that you?" Colonel Colfax called out again.

"Yeah," the man in the cage answered, his voice hoarse. He spoke between gulps of water. "That's my name. Glad you came along. But who the hell are you?"

"Skye Fargo," Scarbelly said under his breath. He spit on the ground. It was clear the major had heard of the famous Trailsman and of his reputation.

"Ben Colfax," the colonel answered, surprised his old friend hadn't recognized him. Maybe he'd lost his mind. "You must remember me. Why we—"

"Yeah, I remember," Fargo cut him off dismissively. "I met you up in Wyoming once. Think you can get me out of here now?"

"Sure," said Colfax, surprised at Fargo's curt tone. "Sure, Fargo. But how—who did this to you?" Colfax asked.

"Paiutes. The goddamn Paiutes," Fargo snapped. "Now, just get me out of here."

As Colonel Colfax dismounted and gave the orders for Scarbelly and Private Bucknell to get Fargo free, he couldn't help but feel disappointment at Fargo's coldness, despite the circumstances. They'd spent a lot of time together up on the Wind River and again on the plains of Kansas. They were old friends. Fargo had saved his life once out in the buffalo fields and now—well, now he was returning the favor.

Fargo, with the aid of Bucknell's knife, had managed to saw through the rawhide that lashed several of the bars of the cage and slipped out of the cage down to the ground. He staggered as he hit the dusty earth. Colonel Colfax swallowed his personal disappointment and adopted a professional tone.

"So, Fargo, you say the Paiutes did this. How many hostiles were there in the band?"

"Twenty braves maybe," said Fargo with a shrug. "I was just passing through taking a shortcut to California and they came on me one night."

"Looks to me like them reds was having a party here," Scarbelly said, kicking one of the animal carcasses.

"They were making sacrifices," said Fargo. "To their war god. I know their language and I heard them talking. They're about to attack every white in the territory. Those damn Paiute savages. I'd like to wipe out every last one of them for putting me up there in that goddamn cage."

"Yeah, now you're talking," said Scarbelly, rubbing his hands together. "I always said the army ought to scalp those reds alive."

"That's right," said Fargo. "Get us some scalps. And I know just where those Paiutes are hiding out. I've seen their trails. I know where their camps are. I say they should just be wiped out once and for all."

Colonel Colfax turned away in confusion. This wasn't the Skye Fargo he'd remembered. What was going on here? And why had the Paiutes put Fargo in that cage anyway?

"You oughtta come back to Fort Ravage and

meet our general," Scarbelly said, slapping Fargo on the back. "Why you and he'd have a lot to talk about. With you knowing where those reds are hiding out, I bet you'd be a real useful man to the general."

"That's enough," Colonel Colfax snapped. He'd heard how the general thought the United States should solve the "Indian problem." He'd heard plenty of people talk that way, including a lot of army men. But wanton killing wasn't official army policy. The official mission of the army was to keep the peace, not incite wars. But now it looked like Skye Fargo himself had gone over to that point of view. He could hardly believe it. He avoided Fargo's gaze and gave the signal for the rest of the soldiers to join them and form up for the return to Fort Ravage. At Colfax's orders, Private Bucknell relinquished his horse to Fargo, supplied him with an extra army shirt from his saddlebag, and doubled up on a horse with one of the other men.

"Fall in," Colfax commanded when they had all assembled. Fargo brought his horse up front alongside the colonel as the rest of the men were drawing up into formation.

"Well, I'm curious to see fort Ravage," said Fargo to Colfax. "I hear it's a real nice place."

Fort Ravage? A *nice* place? The colonel glanced in surprise at Fargo's face. Fargo winked and flashed him a grin, a grin from the old days when they'd ridden together up in the Windy Range, an expression that no one else in the troop could see. And that told Benjamin Colfax everything he wanted to know and more than he imagined he could hope for. No, Skye Fargo hadn't changed. Somehow, someway, Fargo had come here on purpose. Fargo was playing a game—a dangerous game of life and death.

As they rode back to Fort Ravage, Colonel Benjamin Colfax and Fargo didn't exchange another word except what was absolutely necessary. Instead, they treated one another as chance acquaintances, distant companions. Colfax knew that as soon as they found some time alone, his old friend Fargo would explain what the hell was going on. And in return, Colfax would tell him what little he'd found out about the doings at Fort Ravage. With every mile, Colfax felt hope rise in him for the first time since taking on this difficult assignment. With two of them, maybe, just maybe . . .

Meanwhile, Fargo rode at his side on the unaccustomed horse. He felt his muscles loosening after having been tied up in the cage for two days. Yeah, it had been a damn sight uncomfortable. His muscles were stiff, his skin burned by the sun, his lips were cracked with dryness—rubbing them with salt had made them worse of course. But it had only been a day since he'd had his last drink of water and he looked worse than he felt. Sure, there'd been some danger in the plan but it had been worth it. The general and the men at Fort Ravage would fall for it. And as he rode along, he thought back on how he had gotten himself mixed up in this in the first place.